LIAM HOGAN

Happy ending

NOT GUARANTEED

First published in UK 2017 by Arachne Press Limited
100 Grierson Road, London SE23 1NX
www.arachnepress.com
© Liam Hogan 2017
ISBN: 978-1-909208-36-0

Cover, title page and introduction design © Kevin Threlfall
Thanks to Muireann Grealy for her proofing
Printed on wood-free paper in the UK by TJ International, Padstow.

Credits and Copyright

About the Author

Liam Hogan was abandoned in a library at the tender age of three, only to emerge blinking into the sunlight many years later, with a head full of words and an aversion to loud noises.

He's a Liar and co-host of the award-winning monthly literary event, Liars' League, and winner of Quantum Shorts 2015 and Sci-Fest LA's Roswell Award 2016. His steampunk stories appear in Leap Books' 'Beware the Little White Rabbit' #Alice150 anthology, in Flame Tree Publishing's 'Swords&Steam', and in Steampunk Trails II. Science fiction stories appear in DailyScienceFiction, in Sci-Phi Journal, and in Cosmic Roots and Eldritch Shores.

He lives in London, tweets at @LiamJHogan and dreams in Dewey Decimals.

http://happyendingnotguaranteed.blogspot.co.uk/

Acknowledgements

This collection would be a lot slimmer and indeed, wouldn't exist at all, without Liars' League, for whom many of the stories were originally written. A big thanks to Liars' founder and stalwart Katy Darby for her edits on those that were selected and her advice on those that weren't, and to the wonderful actors who brought my stories alive in various rooms in various London pubs.

Thanks also to Cherry Potts of Arachne Press, who published *Rat* and *Palio* in the first Liars' anthology, 'London Lies', and has been a valiant supporter, both of Liars' League and my writing, ever since.

Contents

Happy ending*

This collection of short stories puts its warning in the title. Whether through the inevitable and appalling logic of *Kingdom,* or via the perverse delight of a dark imagination in *Bring Rope*, many of these tales end badly. Deals with the Devil often do, but here deals with Gods and Kings backfire just as tragically.

Of course, that doesn't begin to explain why some of them start badly.

Perhaps I've never trusted tales of mighty heroes. (Somewhere in a mountain shack an old crone stirs. *Heroes*, she spits into the fire.) Or rather, heroes who fail to face a proportionate threat. Even Odin must face Ragnarök and all heroes eventually fall, whether mighty, or meek.

Perhaps I just have a warped mind.

In the interests of full disclosure, I should warn that some of these stories *do* have happy endings. But I won't tell you which in advance. I like to keep you on your toes, keep you guessing as you read. Is this tale going to end horribly, or happily? Happily-*ish*? For the here and now, anyway.

Because Happily Ever Afters are *never* guaranteed: *Tempus edax rerum.*

Consider yourself warned.

If you like your endings happy, Dear Reader, best seek them elsewhere.

NOT GUARANTEED

To Be A Hero

'So,' the crone said, looking up at the tall, muscular man holding a stout cherry-wood pole. 'You want to be a Hero, do you?'

Her cackle was cut short as he shook his head and his wife stepped forward, a cloth-covered bundle in her arms. 'Wise woman,' she said, tugging back the shawl to reveal a sleeping baby, a wisp of pale hair on his crown. 'Please – it is not for us, it is for our son.'

'A long-term project, eh?' the crone chuckled. 'Unswaddle him.'

The woman did as she was asked and the crone took the babe in her lap, holding each tiny hand, each delicate foot, in turn.

'Well. The boy is healthy enough.' She turned and skewered her two visitors with an icy stare. 'If you want your son to be a Hero,' she said, raising a crooked finger and pointing it at them, 'then you will need... to die!'

There was a stunned silence, punctuated by a small cough. 'Excuse me?' the father said.

'Orphans make the best heroes,' she shrugged. 'Everyone knows that.'

'They do?' said the woman, unable to tear her fearful gaze from this aged and quite possibly deranged woman who was clutching her only child.

'From infant wizards and caped crusaders to once and future kings, even Superman: all orphans.' The crone stared at them expectantly.

The woman bit her lip and shook her head, her hand seeking that of her husband.

'Look,' said the man, 'is that strictly necessary?'

'Oh yes,' the crone replied. 'Think about it. What Hero has the chance to run to his mother, who'll comfort him and kiss it all better?

Or can hide behind his father whenever something frightens him?'

The two parents stood in confused thought until the man shook his head. 'I don't think–'

'Well,' the crone cut him off, 'How about if just one of you died?'

'I... erm–'

'–Preferably the mother?'

'The mother?' spluttered the father, tightening his grip on his walking stick.

'That way the father is a distant figure, blaming the infant for the death of the mother in childbirth. Though we might have missed that window of opportunity. Don't worry, sir!' the crone continued, 'you can remarry! As long as the step-mother is particularly mean-spirited and preferably has a brace of her own needy and brutish children.'

'Isn't that Cinderella?' the mother croaked.

'Yes, yes, Cinderella and a dozen others. It works just as well on sons, trust me.'

'I don't think either of us are prepared to die,' the man said, firmly. 'Perhaps if we left him with a distant relative?' he suggested, though the look he got from his wife had him wishing he hadn't.

The crone appeared to think on this. 'No, I'm afraid that won't work. Your son's quest will be to track you down, rather than rescuing fair maidens or fighting fearsome dragons. Also, it leaves the door open for you to return in a moment of high crisis and save the day. Death is preferable.'

Again the two parents frowned and stayed silent. This wasn't going the way they had hoped.

'Suit yourself,' the crone said, 'though it does make the whole "Hero" thing a bit more difficult. Any royal blood in him?'

The two of them shook their heads in concert.

'Pity. An attempt to reclaim a stolen throne usually works quite well. Any prophecies I should be aware of?'

'Erm, no,' admitted the father.

'Hmm.' It was the crone's turn to frown. 'Look, don't take this the wrong way. You seem like nice people and obviously want the best for your son, but are you *sure* you want him to be a Hero?'

'Yes!' exclaimed the father.

'Why?' asked the crone.

'Well... because...' the woman began.

'Because *Hero* is a Great and Noble thing to be!' completed the man. 'Famous deeds, bravery, honour, a chance to win glory!'

'There are many professions that are noble,' pointed out the crone. 'Craftsman, teacher, leader. And "great" is a measure of how well you do your chosen task, however humble.'

The man's face darkened. 'If you won't help us, wise woman, there are others...'

'Oh okay, *fine*. Keep your hair on. I'll see what I can do,' the crone said.

The boy was awake now, his hands clasping and waving around. The crone stuck a couple of fingers into the nearest cauldron and rubbed a white, waxy substance on the infant's dry scalp while it cooed and squirmed in pleasure.

'Is that it?' the woman said doubtfully.

'Is that it?' echoed the crone. 'No! Of course that's not it. You must also... tell your son he is a hero – ah yes! You must tell him that he is "My Hero" whenever he is kind to you or to others. You must feed him well, so that he grows up big and strong. And you must tell him that you love him.'

'Love him?' queried the mother.

'Yes. You do love him don't you?'

The mother and father nodded, as the child gurgled and kicked its legs.

'Then that shouldn't be too difficult. Finally, and this is very, very important, possibly the most important of all, you must allow him to find his own way.'

'And then he'll become a Hero?' asked the father.

'Yes, yes. Of course. He's bound to. Look at the way he's

gripping my finger, a real Hercules in the making. Right, well, I think that's everything.'

'Don't you have a magic sword, or a protective talisman, or something?'

The crone looked at him incredulously. 'A magic sword? No, no... he won't need one of those. In fact, best keep swords and other sharp edges well away from him until he's fully grown. The, um, magic is *within*, and will only be revealed when the time is right.'

'Then thank you, wise woman,' the mother said, bowing her head before eagerly reclaiming her child.

'De nada,' replied the crone.

'How can we repay you?' said the father.

'Think nothing of...' the crone tailed off, thoughtfully. 'What did you have in mind?'

'We don't have much,' admitted the mother.

'But you may take anything you desire,' the father said.

'Anything?' the crone asked, eyeing the man's strong limbs and straight back.

'Anything.'

*

Heroes, she snorted as she poured herself another cup of tea and replaced the lid on the cauldron of freshly prepared cold cream. It was getting harder and harder to convince parents what a stupid idea that was. Sure, heroes made for rousing tales, but role models? *Really?* Misogynistic, brittle-tempered, muscle-brained oafs? Why didn't the parents ask for robust health instead? For happiness? For a solid career path that didn't involve trying to hunt and slay mythical creatures, or to messily hack to death *other* Heroes whose only crime was to be sporting a differently coloured shield?

Ah well, she thought as she cradled the warm cup in her frail hands, at least she'd got a nice new cherry-wood walking stick out of it.

Feathers

Two statues gaze at each other with longing across the London skyline. One perches high above a Victorian telephone exchange, now converted into artists' studios, and is in the image of Mercury, the winged messenger. The other stands proud atop the cupola of a church and represents either one of the nine Muses, or more probably Ariadne; the detailing is rather uncertain.

They talk.

This astounding feat is achieved by means of pigeon. It is a slow, laborious form of communication, but lacking pens or paper they encode their messages the only way they can: by the careful plucking of the wing and tail feathers of captured birds.

We cannot say how it is that they learnt Morse code. We do know that they have been talking for a very long time. Perhaps, though the records do not exist to either confirm or deny this, they shared the same stonemason's yard before being lifted into their exalted positions. Perhaps the lightning conductors and metal pins securing them to their posts picked up the early telegraph signals and radio messages of a once busy shipping city and they learnt by sheer repetition. But then to explain the elaborate error correction necessary in what is a very unreliable messaging system... well, maybe she is a Muse after all.

Nor will we bore you with a detailed description of an average day in their glacially slow lives. The waiting for a pigeon to land, the stealthy capture between lichen-covered fingers, the careful plucking and then release! Only to see the frightened bird vanish into the distance, or worse: plummet to the streets below, the victim of too much information. All in all they manage to exchange a couple of words at most, even on the best of days.

And we will not waste your time asking you to unravel the messages, which, due to the slowness of their communication, inevitably overlap, two sentences flying between them a few letters at a time, such that an answer might arrive before the question is fully posed.

Instead, let us hasten the passage of time so that whole seasons last but a minute and unravel the dits and dahs to relate their tale, in their own words.

'Dear Heart,' proclaimed Mercury. 'My love is as constant as the elements, the rain, the snow, the wind...'

'Really?' replied Ariadne.

'Without doubt, without hesitation!' he insisted.

There was a pause – a fortnight or two – and then: 'Prove it.'

'I would swim rivers for you,' Mercury boasted, amid a flurry of feathers. 'I would climb mountains, scale ravines, battle demons!'

'I don't see you getting any closer,' she retorted.

It was his turn for a silent pause. 'What would you have me do?' he asked, as spring gave way to summer.

'Come to me,' she replied.

'Nothing would please me more!' he exclaimed. 'To move an inch in your direction, to be closer to your divine form, your exquisite beauty, would be sweeter than heaven to me!'

'Then do it.'

'I' – this di-dit was encoded upon a single bird for dramatic emphasis and, for that single bird, constituted a lucky escape – 'cannot.'

'Have you tried?' she asked.

'My feet are firmly bound by metal rods, my legs, in any case, are poorly defined and permanently joined,' he replied with sorrow.

'Where there's a will, there is a way.'

'The climb in itself would be impossible–'

'There's a kiss in it for you.'

'–What?'

'Come here,' she cajoled, 'and I promise you a kiss.'

We can only imagine the thoughts passing through Mercury's solid stone head at this point. We know, from the messages through the years, that he was a romantic. What else could he be? Proclaiming his passion from the rooftops, separated by such a distance from the one he loved? What did he dream of? Did he imagine a day when they might by some miracle be together again, as (perhaps) they were a century earlier in that stonemason's yard?

It was lucky that the first stone fell into an area already cordoned off for road-works and was followed by a cloud of discarded feathers, drawing the eye of the Works' Foreman to the ramparts above, before the second, even larger chunk of masonry crashed to the hastily cleared pavement which, moments before, had thronged with early morning commuters. The taped off area was quickly expanded and grumbling passers-by directed to the opposite side of the street, while the engineers worried that the excavations at street level might somehow have triggered the collapse above and who would get it in the neck as a consequence.

Mercury's last message, 'I love–' never made it across the divide, the over-plucked bird falling easy prey to one London's few hawks. In what to Ariadne appeared the mere blink of an eye, Mercury was surrounded by scaffolding and flapping white sheeting as Health and Safety sprang into action. She gave a wry smile and shifted her attention to the muscle-bound form that was Atlas.

But Atlas didn't know Morse code and even if he had he could not have replied, his bronze arms weighed down by the mighty globe suspended above him. Despite a number of increasingly desperate attempts to attract his attention, his focus remained stubbornly angled down, peering into a busy side street just off Oxford Circus where shop workers gathered for a crafty cigarette and a scaldingly hot Styrofoam coffee.

So when the scaffolding was dismantled and Mercury stood once again in restored splendour, Ariadne tried to rekindle their love, sending messages of entreaty, reminding him of the promises he had once made. Mercury ignored them, and her. His resculpted eyes saw her as she truly was: a crumbling, lonely figure blighted by pollution and droppings and the passage of time, with a heart as cold as stone.

He caught a pigeon for old times' sake and then, with a smile, let it go.

Scarecrow

'There he is,' the farmer nodded.

I looked up to the brow of the hill, where the crucified figure stood against a steel-grey sky, shirt sleeves flapping in the wind.

'And what exactly do you want me to do?' I asked, not for the first time.

The farmer smirked. 'Just touch him. If you dare. I've got twenty says you can't.'

I couldn't see the snag. The ground was muddy from the recent rains, but I'd been through worse. I shrugged and climbed up onto the gate.

'Just touch him?' I asked again.

The farmer rubbed at the stubble on his chin. 'Well now, if you feel that's not enough, I'd be much obliged if you could uproot him and drag him back down here. He's served his time.'

I looked out over the field from my perch. The wheat was ripe, but there wasn't a bird to be seen. I wondered why it hadn't been harvested yet; the neighbouring fields were strewn with bent straw.

I dropped lightly over the other side, a satisfying squelch as my boots took purchase, and started up the hill. It all seemed a bit too easy. Farmers like McGaskill didn't give away their hard-earned money for free. I looked back to where he stood, resting his arms on the gate, and he gave me a cheery wave.

Perhaps there was a bull loose in the field. Just the sort of 'joke' a farmer might try on a townie. I couldn't see one, but that proved nothing. You could have hidden a small battalion behind that hill. I felt my heart pounding and wondered how fast I'd be able to run if push came to shove.

The ground was drier on the slope and I'd just begun to pick up my pace when my army-issue boot struck something. I had a sudden and all-too-vivid image of being thrown through the air, my limbs shredded by an anti-personnel mine or an unexploded cluster bomb. I slowly raised my foot to see the piece of flint hidden beneath.

The wind stroked the wheat, making the heads bend in waves that sped towards the foreboding figure ahead. I scanned the darkening horizon; pretty bloody stupid, marching to the top of a hill in the middle of a storm! My pace slowed even as my brain was telling me to get it over with quickly: touch the scarecrow and back down the hill before the rain and lightning began, to hell with uprooting it, the farmer could do his own dirty work.

I imagined him appraising me from below, seeing my faltering steps, judging me by my weakness. I tugged up the collar of my coat and stamped my feet a couple of times to chase away the feeling of cold.

An odd noise it made, like distant mortars being fired, the whump-whump that were the last sounds you ever heard if they were on target...

But that was crazy! This was rural Bedfordshire, less than a hundred miles from London, not some god-forsaken Afghan hell-hole! And yet I could feel the hairs on my neck stand on end and my breath caught in my throat. Perhaps the farmer was just plain psycho and was waiting with a double barrelled shotgun until I was silhouetted against the sky. He'd seemed sane enough, if a little taciturn, in the pub last night. Until his eyes lit up when he heard I was ex-services and he'd casually suggested I drop by his farm on my way out of the village.

Maybe it was the land itself. What might be buried beneath the soil? Burnt carcasses from the BSE epidemic? Anthrax spores? Or a mass grave from a Viking raid, bodies with arms tied tightly behind their backs before being dispatched with cruel blows of sword or axe?

I shook the images from my head. You wouldn't farm on contaminated land and if it was some ancient burial mound, well what of it? The bones were hardly able to hurt me now.

I must have been about half way up that bleak and desolate hill, when I ground to a halt once more, raising my hand above my eyes to get a better look at what lay ahead. I was approaching the scarecrow from behind. It wore tattered trousers and a jacket with the arms half rolled up, leaving the shirt sleeves free to flutter about the wooden pole. The head was made of straw beneath a grey cap, but it almost looked like there was hair there as well. Christ! Maybe it wasn't made of straw at all. Maybe it was a corpse, left to dry in the wind, its heart rattling around an empty chest, its eyes rotted and–

Goddamnit! Anyone would think that I was a little kid, listening wide-eyed and open-mouthed to ghost stories around the camp fire. It was just a scarecrow, an inanimate object to frighten away the birds, not grown men, not me. I slowly took another half step forward.

Maybe... maybe it was better if I just asked the farmer what the catch was? He could hardly refuse to tell me, could he? I was in no fit state to negotiate the hazard, whatever it might be; my heart was racing, my back was slick with sweat, and my left leg trembled as if it had a mind of its own and was busy remembering past injuries, past nightmares. I should ask...

And then I was marching, almost skipping, back down the hill, at full speed, grateful for every step I took away from the dark shape behind me. As I neared the gate I slowed, suddenly wary of the farmer's reaction, but he just stood there white faced, without a trace of a grin. He held out a dull grey hip flask which I gratefully received, taking a good gulp of the fiery liquid, before hopping back over the fence.

The farmer eyed me narrowly. 'It sure is something, isn't it?' he asked.

I nodded slowly, uncertain exactly what he meant.

19

'If it's any consolation, that's further than I, or anyone else from the village got.' He rubbed his hand on the back of his neck. 'Even tried to take the tractor up there, flatten the bugger, but, well. We'll pass it on the way.'

I followed him along the edge of field. We stopped at a gate. 'Look,' he said, pointing down to some seed that had been spilled on the ground. It formed a neat line exactly where the gate passed over it. 'All the seed on this side of the fence, gone. Eaten by the birds, or mice, or whatever. All the seed on that side of the fence, untouched. Not a single bloody bird, they won't even fly over the field.' He shook his head. 'This is the gate I tried to drive the tractor through.'

There were a set of tram lines through the crop, initially heading straight up the hill, then quickly wavering, before veering dramatically off to one side. I craned my head over the fence and saw the tractor wedged at an angle in the hedge some twenty or so yards further along.

'I was lucky not to kill myself; felt the tractor tip as I wrenched the wheel. Not sure how I got through the hedge, it's all a bit of a blur, but the tractor isn't coming out that way. Not unless I cut the hedge down, which I've thought of doing, then I suppose I could tow it,' he mused.

'I don't understand,' I said. 'What's causing all of this?'

He turned and stabbed his blunt fingers up the hill. 'That thing. That bloody scarecrow. "Best scarecrow you'll ever have", the gypsy said. "Guaranteed bird free."' The farmer spat. 'Nobody and nothing has been able to enter the field since he put it up. And now all that wheat's going to go to waste. Damn. I shouldn't really have expected you to do any better.'

I bristled at this; hadn't I got further than anyone else? But how far had I got? Not much more than half way up the hill, that's for sure. 'I could get your tractor for you,' I said.

He turned, a pained expression on his face. 'Yes? You sure about that?'

I trembled and suddenly realised I couldn't. Not today, anyway.

'Thought as much. Thanks for the offer, though.' He gazed off into the distance and I hung my head. 'Look, I shouldn't have done that to you. It was mean. But I could hardly tell you, could I? Had to let you try on your own. Ah damn. Will you come back to the house? There's hot soup on the stove.'

We trudged in silence to the small farmyard. I felt drained, cold and weary, my mind numb. But as the farmer pushed the heavy wooden door aside a border collie leapt up at us and I felt the warmth of the stove even from the kitchen door.

'Daft pup,' the farmer said, as he stroked the dog's head affectionately. 'Only six months old and ain't a patch on his mother, but there you go. Refuses to leave the farmyard, never mind going anywhere near the scary man on the hill. Maybe not so daft after all. Make yourself at home, man, I'll get you a bowl.'

I shed the jacket and thought about removing my muddy boots, but McGaskill wasn't removing his, so I left them on. I sat on a wooden bench at the rough table and he brought out a hunk of bread on a chopping board before plonking something more like a stew than a soup before me. I ate ravenously, feeling the warmth and energy flow back.

'Have you tried shooting it down?' I asked.

He shook his head. 'You can't get a steady aim on the thing. Even from outside of the field. Not that my shotgun would do any damage from there.'

'Burning it?' I said between mouthfuls.

'Hah! Well that would get rid of it, but it'd take out the whole crop as well. Besides, you can't even burn stubble these days without a permit.'

I thought for a moment. 'What about the gypsy?' I asked.

'What about him?' the farmer said with disdain.

'Have you tried to find him? Surely he'd be able to take the scarecrow down?'

'No doubt he could, at a price,' the farmer replied. 'Which hell, I'd be willing to pay. But they don't exactly leave a forwarding address. Best I can hope is that he'll be back next spring. But that'll be two crops wasted, it'll be too late to sow by then.'

'Won't it seed itself?' I asked.

He snorted. 'It might. But it won't weed itself. It'll be okay maybe for animal feed, but nowt else.'

I was silent, gears whirring in my brain, but with little effect.

'You done?' the farmer asked.

'Err, yes. Thanks.' I handed him my empty bowl. 'Look, I'm sorry...'

He shook his head. 'Don't be. You did ya best. My own stupid fault. Never trust a tinker.'

At the door I shouldered my pack. 'Best be getting on,' I said, as I ruffled the neck of the border collie.

The farmer nodded. 'Where next?'

I shrugged, suddenly unable to meet his eye. 'Northampton,' I replied. It wasn't on my route, but the thought of another two weeks hiking, even if it was for charity, left me cold. 'Walk for Heroes'. Some hero I'd turned out to be. A small detour, to somewhere with pubs and people and rooms with showers, wouldn't upset my plans too much if I did decide to continue.

And even though my pack was heavy and my gammy leg complained bitterly, I left the farmyard at a brisk jog. I didn't even look back, averting my eyes from the brow of the hill as I passed, eager to put some miles between me and that damned scarecrow.

Greenwich, Noon

I know when it is noon.

Though I am blind and dumb and kept in a small cell in the rafters of the Royal Observatory, I *know* when it is noon.

I know because at precisely that time a retired ship's surgeon will carve the day's date into my flesh. Each letter, each numeral, is a series of slashes of the knife. He cuts swiftly, with precision. The wound is then sprinkled with the "powder of sympathy", a pungent, acrid substance which reacts violently with my tortured skin and burns, and burns, and burns.

The surgeon, I think, is glad that I cannot scream.

Half way round the world, they hope that the deep cuts they make in me are felt by my twin sister. We are part of a sea trial, she and I, an attempt to claim the prize promised by the Longitude Act of 1714. Her role as the seafaring twin was decided for her because she, though as blind as I am, can cry out as I cannot, and so alert the distant sailors aboard the schooner *Regina*, that it is noon here in Greenwich. By comparing this with their own, local noon, they will then know their longitude.

So goes the theory.

The sea trial will be deemed a failure, a relief perhaps to any other twins born to our abject poverty and equally lacking in those attributes by which they might otherwise be deemed human. For we are referred to not as people, but as dogs. That is how we are seen: two worthless lives, two souls so damaged from birth that until this cruel experiment began, we weren't even given names.

Now, they call me Sirius, after the dog star.

They call my sister Venus, the brightest of the wandering

stars. They imagine her wandering across the oceans, looking to the dog star to know her place upon this Earth.

You must wonder how it is that I know what I know; how it is that I can even tell my story, when I lack the senses you take so easily for granted.

You assume, as does the surgeon, that because I am dumb I am also *deaf*.

You assume that because I cannot see, I cannot *write*.

I have learnt the shape of your words. With my fingers I have traced the rough edges of the scars they leave on my skin. These have been hard lessons, every word carries the pain of cutting it into my flesh; this is how I order my thoughts, by the long, sharp strokes of an L, by the twist that tugs at the skin for the curve of a C, by the swift back and forth of an S. Each letter I know by how it feels to have it inscribed upon me, the lesson reinforced by the searing agony of the caustic powder with which my wounds are liberally sprinkled.

I am ignored by the surgeon, and by the two who throw rancid food into my cell and who all too rarely sweep the soiled straw from it. They are carefree with their words, these fools, for what does it matter what is said in front of one who cannot repeat what they say?

I think back to when my sister and I shared a filthy, infested bed in the hell in which we were raised, a hell that I now long to return to. She would croon to me, her awkward voice a balm against the kickings and the abuse that was always there, always sudden and always unforeseen.

When we were brought for the first time to Greenwich, and, for the first time, separated, I could still hear her through the thin walls of our cells, and I was not as concerned as I should have been.

And when she cried out in pain, when some terrible injury was done to her, I shared that pain, and thrashed and jerked in mutual torment. To the evident satisfaction of the great and good men there present.

If only I had stayed still, our fate might have been different and she would not be lost to me now.

My cell is quiet, when there is only me in it. If I lie still I can hear the conversations happening next door, or below. There is a great space there; once a week a crowd throngs, a meeting of the Commissioners of the Discovery of the Longitude at Sea, and the voices of the speakers are raised above the din of the multitude. From them I have learnt of the Prize that condemned my sister and me.

They talk about it incessantly, one crazed scheme after another. Sometimes they mention the *Regina*, and I know that these men, for all their fine learning and long words, do not know what I know: that the *Regina* will never return home, that it moulders at the bottom of the ocean.

I know this, because I have felt it. When my body was only half as scarred as it is now, I awoke breathless and panicky, a feeling that only intensified as I struggled to suck down the dank night air, as my bloodied hands beat upon the floor, until suddenly a bucket of my own filth was thrown over my shuddering form, a gaoler laughing at my plight. As the cold, rank liquid dripped off my face, I knew with more certainty than I have ever known anything before; that whatever small space my sister was confined to aboard the *Regina* it was flooded, and my sister was drowning.

I felt her anguish in every part of me, across the miles of ocean and land, I felt the pressure and the burning flames in her lungs as the ship surely sank.

Afterwards, as I sat huddled in a corner while my gaoler spat and kicked, I was consumed by an emptiness that hollowed me out from within, and I knew that for the first time ever, I was truly alone.

I could not comprehend why the surgeon still came the next day, and the next. How could he not feel it too? How could he not know?

The *Regina* is overdue. Fourteen months it has been gone. There are few parts of me left that remain unmarked by the passage of time, by the surgeon's knife. But still he keeps coming. Every day the surgeon cuts the date into me, sending an unheeded message to the bottom of the sea that it is noon here in Greenwich.

Today is the last such day.

Though I am blind, I hear the key in the lock as the surgeon opens the door, his footsteps as he approaches across the wooden floorboards. I know how long it takes between the lifting of the rags that cover me and the first cut of the knife. I smell his stale sweat and feel his hot breath and steel myself. The surgeon rests the point of the knife where he will make his first cut and exhales to steady his aim. With my left hand that I have wriggled free of my bonds, I reach out and seize his wrist, and with my other I twist and slam the sharp blade into his exposed throat.

I wait until I can no longer hear the drumming of his heels on the straw-strewn floor before I withdraw the knife. It does not take long.

Though I am mute, I inscribe my story – this story – for all to read, whether by sight or by touch, onto the body of the surgeon. I swiftly slash each neat letter, feeling the splash of the still warm blood spill onto my fingers, hearing the drip to the wooden boards at my feet. I hope, I *pray*, that it will drip all the way through to the congregation gathered in the great space below, as they sit there discussing balloons and cannon ships and the moons of Jupiter, and let those learn'd men know, that it is noon, here, in Greenwich.

The Giant, Snow-White

Yes, there were seven of us. Seven *People*. Oh, and her, the giant, Snow-White.

Most folk don't have a name for themselves. They have names for everyone else. To us, we're just *The People* and no, I really, really don't want to hear your name for us.

Anyway, this story you *already* know. That's not what happened. It ain't exactly complimentary. Fights break out when it's told in our company. And we might not be giants, but we're lethal in a melee. Though we may not be able to cut your throats, there are plenty of vital parts we damn well can reach.

Look, I'm just saying, keep an open mind. That other tale, it's going to colour your imagination. Stories do that, good ones as well as bad. So sit back and listen, but keep your god-damn interruptions to yourself, or I'll be up a stepladder so fast you'll never know what got your tongue.

Some tales begin with an origin. Three drops of blood on snow, blah, blah, blah... The boring truth is that seven is the usual number for miners. Three at the rock face, three to shift rubble and one to keep an eye on the canary. Happens I was the canary watcher.

You're trying to guess my name now, aren't you? Even though they didn't bloody well *have* names in the Brothers Grimm version all your stories are descended from, you still want to square my tale with the stupid names Disney used for 'comic' effect?

Damn it. Fine. My name is... Blossom.

Settle down. Settle *right* down. It's a lot more manly in our language, believe you me. Anyone who wants to discuss the matter further, I'll be waiting, outside, afters.

So we seven miners are minding our own business, our business being the extraction of high-grade iron ore, when this giant does a breaking-and-entering on our mountain cabin.

You could tell she wasn't the smartest cookie. You don't break into a miner's cabin – especially one where you have to bend double to get through the door – and expect a warm welcome.

We let her stay because it was obvious she was desperate. And because all her caterwauling was seriously messing with the wind-down after a hard day's mining. We had to promise her *something* just to shut her up. She spilled some sob story of begging for her life from an axe-wielding huntsman, but, you know? That's what happens when step-mothers with ambition become Queen and it's got nothing to do with jealousy or beauty. And despite what you may have heard, Snow-White was no looker. 'Fairest of them all'? Pfft! She didn't even have a beard. No, it's simple heredity politics. Bit like a cuckoo. Not even original.

And not so easily escaped from either.

We tried to warn her, really we did. We knew the old Queen wouldn't give up just like that. But, like I said, Snow-White wasn't the sharpest. Once we'd trotted back to the rock face early next morning – and no, there was absolutely no Heigh-Ho-ing, not in an avalanche zone – what does Snow-White do but let in the first thinly disguised pedlar who just 'happens' to wander by?

Finding a giant sprawled on your kitchen floor not breathing is enough to turn a beard grey, but we managed to get Snow-White out of that particular sorry mess with a quick bit of bodice ripping and some mouth-to-mouth. I'm not at liberty to tell which of us seven – Doc, you say? No, there was no 'Doc' there. Yes, I'm *quite* sure. You done with your heckling, boyo?

To think, a whale had to die so that a chubby girl could get an hour glass figure. Maybe we'd have been a bit more careless with the dagger we ran between those stays if we'd known that wasn't going to be the end of it. If it wasn't an over-tightened corset, it was a poisoned comb and if it wasn't a poisoned comb, it was a rosy red, venom drenched apple.

That one stumped us, because who'd believe a girl with three near-as-damn-it successful attempts on her life, would be idiot enough to take food from yet another stranger? None of us thought to look down the damn fool girl's damn fool gullet.

It was sheer luck that some namby-pamby Prince came mincing by and offered to take her comatose body off our hands. And we were glad to be rid of her, because by then we were fed up of standing guard and shooing away the birds. Mostly crows, which is never a particularly good sign of health. It was costing us valuable time and the mountain mining season is damnably short.

Lucky as well that the Prince was such a clumsy klutz. He manhandled Snow-White so rudely that she up-chucked the slice of vilely poisoned apple.

Naturally, after a bit of cleaning up and rest assured, Princess vomit is just as foul as anyone else's, the two upper-class twits hit it off splendidly and rushed away to get hitched. Bloody ingrates. We didn't even get an invite to the wedding and by all accounts, it was a doozy.

Still, it wasn't a total bust. We People came out on top. We usually do, for all that we have further to climb. Who was it, do you think, that provided the high-grade iron for the old Queen's new pair of red-hot boots?

Blaxley And Whiteclaw

Edmund chewed the ends of the moustache he'd been growing since we were wed. It wasn't really long enough, not yet; the thin wisps kept escaping the attentions of his lips, but he didn't seem to notice. He looked up through bushy eyebrows darkened by an unfamiliar frown. Or rather, a frown unfamiliar to him.

'You look like your dad,' I said, and he did, especially now that he had started to let his beard grow. True, he hadn't the barrel chest and his arms, muscular though they were, weren't quite so prodigious, nor as scarred, as his father's. But it was clear: in a dozen years or so, he'd look just the same. The anvil forged more than mere metal.

'Emily, are you sure you're good with this? I wouldn't ask, but...'

I rested my hand on his broad shoulder, gave the solid flesh a squeeze, smiling at the thought that for once, it was I who towered over him, albeit from the saddle of the smithy's elderly pack horse, Conkers. 'I'm *fine*, Eddie,' I said, not for the first time. 'It's only an hour's ride–'

'–And you know the way, yes?'

'Yes, yes, I know the way. Haven't I been there with you twice before? Now, husband mine, quit your worrying and get back to your work!'

He nodded, as if in solemn agreement. 'Ride carefully, my love.'

'I will,' I promised as I coaxed the ageing bay into motion.

By the time I took the turn-off into the woods, the fresh smell of young nettles thick around me, I could hear the double ring of hammer on steel as father and son struck and counter-struck, the rhythm outpacing even that of shod hooves on the packed earth.

The noise faded as the trees closed in. Just the clop-clop of the old horse and my thoughts for company. It would be unlikely that I would see any other travellers; the smithy was out of sight of the rest of town – the noise and smoke made for reluctant neighbours – and the path I was taking was rarely frequented.

As I swayed in the saddle my cargo was silent behind me. It had been well packed, as it deserved to be. Each blade was individually wrapped in coarse cloth to protect the keen edges. The dozen swords represented nearly six months' labour for the two blacksmiths, or more accurately, swordsmiths: Edmund, my husband of less than a year; and my father-in-law, the iron-hewed Albert Blaxley, the taciturn patriarch.

The swords would sell well at the tourney that was fast approaching. Knights and merchants from the breadth of the kingdom would be there, as much for the market set up in the grounds of the Duke's castle as for the sport.

But they would not sell as they were, for all that they were fine pieces of steel. Despite their perfect balance, the simple elegance of their cross guards, the grip of their ribbed hilts, they would only become truly desirable once they had been to the Lady Whiteclaw, once she had worked her eldritch magic over them.

Blaxley and Whiteclaw, already the brand was beginning to make a name for itself: superior forged steel with a panoply of protective spells and incantations. All being well, the load I was carrying would set the four of us up for the rest of the year.

Not that the smiths would likely slacken off even so, not that anyone knew what the Lady Whiteclaw did with her half-share.

The pack horse plodded steadily on. This was a journey that had been planned for a long time, to coincide with the rarity of a local tourney, a chance to cut out the middleman, to fully reap the rewards of the hard work through the winter months.

But it had not been meant for today and it was not meant to be me who travelled alone to the sorceress.

Her message had been delivered by crow, the thin roll of

parchment coaxed from the grip of its black talons with a scratch under the chin and a crust from the breakfast table. I suspected it would have freely delivered its small load without such inducements, but I saw no reason to skimp on the hospitalities.

The Lady Whiteclaw had been called for, the message said: an unscheduled convocation of her sisters. She would be away for perhaps as long as a month. If the Blaxleys wanted the final stage of their sword-making completed before the upcoming tourney, they needed to send their stock to her today.

Albert had listened as I read the note aloud. 'It must be done,' he said after a moment's thought.

Edmund waved at the already lit forge. 'But the Duke's commission...'

I'd watched them work together long enough to know why he was so torn. Like the swords, the commission – an ornate candelabra – had to be ready for the tourney, itself a celebration of the Duke and Duchess's fruitful ten-year marriage. Today the large individual pieces would be assembled, welded and riveted into place, a job for two smiths. Tomorrow, and perhaps for the rest of the week, the metal would be smoothed and polished and engraved, detailed work that required only one craftsman at a time, freeing up Edmund for the ride to the Lady Whiteclaw.

Tomorrow, though, the Lady Whiteclaw would be gone.

'I'll go,' I said, and the frown had made its first appearance on my husband's brow. 'I'll go,' I repeated, with more confidence.

Albert had simply nodded, the solution acceptable to him, before turning his attention back to the forge.

For all of Edmund's concern, I was glad of the chance to escape, even if only for a little while. The may was in full flower, it was the first fine day of spring and the thought of spending it in the heat of the smithy, working the bellows or fetching cold drinks for the two labouring men, was less than attractive.

Besides, why shouldn't it be me? I was part of the family now and a blacksmith's wife did not baulk at a short ride through the woods, even woods as untamed as these.

Though I wished I'd brought along a shawl. It was cooler than I'd hoped for among the shadows of the trees, the still unfurling leaves permitting only occasional glimpses of the blue sky dotted with cotton-tufted clouds. But it couldn't be far now.

If there's a problem with riding alone, it's that there's no-one to slap down any dark thoughts. I peered along the path, not recognising anything. Though what was there to recognise? One stretch of path and trees looked much like any other.

Or perhaps... Was this *the* path? Had I, somewhere along the way, turned off? Or missed a turning?

But that was daft, there was only one path, wasn't there? I racked my brains, trying to remember the previous times I'd come this way. Edmund had led the horse and I'd done little more than follow, hanging off Edmund's free arm, paying more attention to my husband-to-be than to my surroundings.

The way opened up onto a small clearing and my worries took on a keener edge. Surely I'd remember this? A woodland glade, carpeted with vibrant spring flowers, alive with the promise of summer?

In the centre sat the blackened remains of a once mighty oak, struck, presumably, by lightning. Had it happened this winter past? Perhaps the clearing hadn't been there in August, when last I made the journey.

I tugged at the reins, urging Conkers forward.

She didn't move. The clearing was eerily quiet, the chirp and flutter of courting birds, the willow lark and the bramble jay that had accompanied me thus far, now conspicuously silent. A chill raised the hairs on my bare arms and I dug my heels hard into the side of my reluctant mount.

This time the bay snorted, her ears pricked up as she swayed her head from side to side.

I craned around, trying to see what had got her spooked. The unwelcome thought sprang to mind that I was carrying a valuable cargo. A young women alone and in charge of a small fortune. True, the swords would be even more valuable on my return, but who but I knew that?

These were peaceful times, I told myself. There had been no reports of any trouble, not even through the long winter, when people sometimes turned in desperation to things they would not normally do.

Though didn't Albert always say that if the times were truly peaceful, there would be no need for swords at all?

I snapped to the right as I caught movement, peered past the pool of sunlight into shadows. There! Beneath a swaying branch; was that the glint of a pair of yellow eyes?

Animal, then. And not alone, either: another glint, from my left this time, also lurking in the low brush at the darkened edges of the clearing. The fact that they were not human gave me little comfort.

As the pack horse stood, dark mane quivering, I snuck my hand towards the roll behind my saddle. Could I extract a sword without untying the leather straps?

I risked a glance behind me and when I looked back the eyes had gone. Or perhaps I had imagined them all along.

'You are looking for me?'

Between two trees, a pale hand resting lightly on one of them, stood the Lady Whiteclaw. Tall and thin, her ash white cloak almost sparkled, for all that she was in shadow.

'There was...' I gestured to where the eyes had lingered, my breath short.

'Never mind them,' she said, taking a step into the clearing. 'Emily Gladwin, isn't it?'

'Blaxley. It's Emily Blaxley, now.'

She raised an eyebrow, took in the bundle strapped behind me. 'So. You have brought the swords?'

I nodded, relieved. 'Shall I ride on to your dwelling?'

'Here is as good a place as any,' she said, and clucked quietly.

A silver horse nosed its way into the clearing, dipped its head as if in greeting. It was a stunning sight: 16 hands high, athletic, as elegant as Lady Whiteclaw herself and seemingly sparkling just as she did. It made Conkers look like the tired old nag she was. I patted the coarse brown hair on her neck as she snickered and tossed her head towards the white mare.

Dismounting, I fumbled with the straps, eager to see the Lady work her magic. The times before this, I had remained with the pack horse, whiling away the hour or so until Edmund returned, the swords rewrapped, the magic done, jealous of what he had been privy to behind the plain wooden door of the enchantress's simple cottage.

I knew a little of what she did. When we had returned to the smithy, Eddie had reverently shown how, with the right words, the blades could be coaxed to glow in the dark. He told me that the edge was now more resilient, protected from damage by a spell that bound all parts of the sword together, a process that mimicked and reinforced the folding and flattening that the two smiths exacted with fire and hammer. A bewitched blade would take a lot of punishment before it shattered into a hundred pieces.

There were other things too: a tip that would change colour if dipped in poison. The blade could be used to divine for water, or to point towards the North Star even on a cloudy night.

He saved the best until last. He had me hold the blade, showed me where to tap to make it hum, and as I held it, listening to the note that refused to die away, the other enchanted swords in the rack nearby began to murmur, as if they sang in chorus. A friend or foe enchantment: the same technique would produce a discord if done near the swords of those who would be enemies, even if hidden.

I lifted the heavy bundle and carefully lowered it to the ground. Edmund had done this in reverse with one hand, as though it was a mere bundle of firewood, using the other to do up the straps, but then, I wasn't Edmund.

Rolling the blanket out, I displayed the shrouded forms contained within, six hilts to the left, six to the right. A couple were a foot longer than the others, the rest the exact same length.

'Unwrap one,' the Lady ordered.

I did as I was told, feeling the cold, smooth metal. There was supposedly an inlay, towards the cross-guard, the letters B and W: the mark that showed who had crafted these swords. I wondered by what magic it would be revealed.

I brought it to her, held the blade horizontal, resting it lightly on my palms like an offering.

She took it carefully, held it aloft in the air, her eyes lightly closed. I could see her lips moving in silent incantation.

Before I knew it she had thrust the sword deep into the mossy floor. She couldn't be done already, could she? I marvelled that for this moment's work she was paid half the price each sword would bring.

'Another!' she ordered.

I handed her one of the longer blades, a horse sword: a hand and a half. It was not much heavier than the other finely constructed blades, but the extra reach made it suitable for a mounted knight, or if dismounted, with one hand firmly behind the pommel, it could be thrust through thin chain mail. No wonder they were sometimes called bastard swords.

She ran two of her fingers over it, as if feeling for a pulse, and then plunged it into the earth along with the first.

'Another!' she barked again, a frown creasing her forehead. For a moment, the shine that seemed to linger on her pale skin faded.

'There's something wrong with the swords, isn't there?' I asked.

She looked across at me, then nodded. 'Do you know, Emily Blaxley, why the smithy is located at the very edge of town?'

'The noise?' I suggested.

'The magic.'

I shook my head. Artistry, yes, hard work, definitely, but it was hard to imagine anything created with less magical input. 'The Blaxleys–'

'–The Blaxleys don't have a magical bone in their bodies,' she finished for me. 'And that, dear girl, is the point. Freshly forged metal is sensitive to the slightest of magical vibrations, it soaks them up like a damp cloth. For me to impress my spells on these swords, for those enchantments to be direct of purpose, single minded, as the swords of men are required to be, it must be kept away from all magical sources until the time is right. Once I have cast my spells, the blades are protected as much from other magic as from wear and tear.'

She reached across, patted the blanket with its collection of still wrapped blades. 'These swords are not the blank templates I was expecting.'

There was silence as I absorbed this startling information. 'How?'

'*Who?* is the more interesting question. As to the *how*: the signal is weak, unfocused. It is most likely accidental. But it must be understood.'

'You think there is someone magical in the village?'

'Oh, I suspect someone much closer to home.'

I felt a chill under the gaze of her pale grey eyes. 'You don't... you don't think it's me?'

'These are the first swords produced while you have been living under the Blaxley roof, are they not?'

'But I've been on this trip before. Twice!'

'Yes, I know. And, as I said, it is a faint trace. It is hard to get a handle on it. I hope it will become clearer back at the smithy.'

Something tore at my insides. How could this be? I wasn't magical. Like every other girl, I'd been tested at the age of eleven, had my childish dreams shattered, again like every other girl. Only one in a thousand was ever selected to be trained, to learn how to boost those rare, nascent powers, to harness them until they became strong enough to be useful.

As I grew older, I realised I'd had a lucky escape. I did not envy Lady Whiteclaw's abilities, not after I saw how most in the village feared her.

There was a reason, as remote as the smithy was, that Lady Whiteclaw's cottage was even remoter.

'Will that not delay your departure?' I asked.

She called her ghost of a horse to her and it came without hesitation. 'The smithy is on my way. And besides, this may be important.'

I began to wrap the swords back up, before I remembered the two stuck into the soft forest floor. I extracted the hand-and-a-half, using a cloth to gently smooth away the smear of dirt and moss. But as I was about to pull out the shorter blade a light grip on my shoulder stopped me.

'I'll carry this one,' she said, plucking it from the soil.

The Lady rode bare back, there were no reins, no bit, and yet her mount was under perfect control. It had a coiled energy that had me urging my horse on until she called out: 'Let Conkers be. She'll find her own pace.'

I was nervous. The day had not gone as expected and I worried about the reaction when I returned to the smithy, with swords no more magical than when I had departed.

The Lady did nothing to allay my fears. We rode in silence, though twice I got the impression that something was tracking our passage and once, through a gap in the canopy above, I glimpsed a gliding silhouette, the splayed wing-feathers and blocky fantail of some large bird of prey, a kite, or a goshawk, perhaps.

I caught voices even before I saw the fading smoke from the forge, and the pang hit me hard. They were bright and manly. The comradely voices of two men, no ladyfolk about, their hard work nearing completion.

And here came I, to dampen their spirits and crush their plans. For a moment, I wondered how far Conkers would be willing to take me, how I might survive away from this new home of mine, a home that I had left with such foolish eagerness a scant hour or two earlier.

The Lady reached across and placed a hand on mine. 'Have courage, Emily Blaxley. All will be well.'

I nodded, steeling myself as the smiths' conversation abruptly stopped.

'Emily?' Edmund looking up from the trough he had obviously just plunged his still dripping head into.

'Lady Whiteclaw,' his father nodded.

'Albert,' the Lady acknowledged.

'I did not expect—'

'No, nor I.' She slid off the back of her horse, still holding that first sword in one hand.

I fidgeted, head bowed as she explained the situation. I tuned out the words and heard only the emotions, the smiths' surprise, their doubt, their concerns, nerves building in me until Edmund's hand sought mine and I breathed out deeply, reassured by his firm grip.

'There is still call for unprotected blades,' the Lady said, into the silence that met the end of her telling. 'Religious orders, for example.'

Edmund frowned, while Albert nodded. 'And there is other metalwork than swords,' he said.

'There is,' she agreed, pointing at the candelabra awaiting its polishing, 'And you have the skills for it. However...'

She reached beneath her cloak, plucked a leather purse, threw it casually onto the rough table. 'That is for this sword, which I shall carry to the convocation.'

Neither swordsmith pointed out that she had paid the amount an enchanted sword would garner, nor that half that price would have been hers anyway.

'But this magical trace,' Edmund said, 'how do we shield against it?'

The Lady laughed. 'You don't. Only distance protects against such unfocused power.'

Edmund's hand slipped from mine, which fluttered as I tucked it back against my shivering body. I looked up through tears, his unintentional message clear. He even took a half-step away, as a sob threatened to escape me. Only distance...

'But I think you may be jumping too quickly to your conclusions,' the Lady said into the awkward silence. 'Even now I do not know where the magic comes from.'

'So,' Albert grunted, 'how do we find out?'

I remembered the tests I had endured at the tender age of eleven, the probing and the questions and the noxious brew that had turned my stomach, and shuddered.

The Lady moved to the apple tree that stood by the trough. In autumn it produced large numbers of small, bitter fruit, fruit that were bartered with the local pig farmer for a side of winter bacon, the flesh fattened on this late crop. For now, small new leaves cluttered around hard little buds of blossom, still tightly curled.

She plucked a silver knife and cut three branches, holding them in her hands for a moment before passing one to each of us.

There was a warm tingle, a sensation of breathing in and out through my fingertips. My eyes widened as the red buds unfurled to become white flowers tinged with pink.

'But I can't be!' I exclaimed, feeling lightheaded, looking up and seeing that the two smiths' branches remained unchanged, seeing their gaze on me, seeing... what? 'The tests?!'

'Did I mention I knew your grandmother?' Lady Whiteclaw said with a smile.

I shook my head, distracted. I'd always assumed Lady Whiteclaw was not far off our age, Edmund and I. Older, for sure, though not by more than a dozen years. But my grandmother had passed long before I was born and was not talked of. Now that I took a closer look, there were undoubtedly fine lines across the Lady's forehead and at the edges of those grey eyes, which glittered as she met my gaze.

'She was a remarkable woman,' she said. 'It isn't uncommon for the magic to skip a generation, almost as though it was drawing breath, but it is rarer for it to skip two.'

'Two?' I echoed dumbly.

The Lady Whiteclaw gently pulled the short branch from my fingers, laying a delicate hand against my midriff.

'Dear girl, the magic is not yours. It is your unborn child's.'

'My child's?' I gasped, looking to Edmund, and he looked back in equal surprise. 'But I'm not... I haven't even missed my period.'

'You will. And it will be a daughter, a powerfully magical one, by the signs of this. I have not heard tell of such a thing before. I had wondered that the trace was so faint, I should instead have marvelled that it was so strong.'

Edmund's frown changed into a smile and then a small laugh, as Albert thumped him between the shoulders.

The Lady looked at me, reappraising. 'You have some schooling, do you not, Emily?'

I nodded. 'I can read.'

'Good,' she said. 'That will come in handy.'

'I don't– but I don't know how...' I fumbled. To raise a child...

I had dreamt of this, wished for it, though perhaps not quite so soon. I had imagined in a year or two, as Edmund stepped into the role his father as yet showed no signs of relinquishing, as our fortunes improved.

Edmund and Albert continued to hug, the older man's face creased with laughter. I did not understand the blacksmith's reactions. A child: another mouth to feed, one that even before she showed in the rounding of my belly had deprived us of our main source of income. And yet the smiths were overjoyed. I found myself smiling in confused echo and then gasped once again as Edmund took hold around my waist and spun me until I was dizzy.

His eyes suddenly widened and he came to an abrupt halt. 'I

shouldn't be doing that, should I?' he said, worry etched across his reddened face.

'Edmund Blaxley,' I told him, blinking away tears, my forehead resting against his, my arms wrapped around his damp neck, 'I am no delicate flower to be swaddled and protected and... and not kissed!'

When I looked up, the Lady Whiteclaw was stood by her horse, dazzlingly bright in the sunlight. She swung up onto its high back, an effortless move I would not have been able to mimic even with saddle and stirrup, even without the gleaming sword she had tucked into a wide, pale-leather belt beneath her loose cloak.

'I'll be back within a month,' she said, as the silver mare swung round to face the road through the village. 'Do not fear, Emily Blaxley. I will be here for you, throughout the pregnancy – and after.'

She rubbed a thin finger against her lips. 'This child of yours, I wonder if *she* is the reason this convocation has been called? If that is indeed the case, then the amount I have paid for a blade touched by her is far less than its true worth.'

She smiled and looked down at the three of us. 'You have an interesting eight months ahead of you – all of you.'

And then, in a thunder of hooves and with the throaty *caw* of a midnight shade that swooped after her from the crown of the nearest tree, she was gone.

Internet Dating For Immortals

George sat on the park bench, holding his head in his hands. He'd already turned away a couple of concerned passers-by, assuring them, between sobs, that he would be all right.

And he would, he knew. Experience told him that. But it didn't make it any easier. It was always tough saying goodbye.

It hadn't helped that he'd broken one of his cardinal rules. Seven years: that was his limit, no relationship to last longer than that. But he'd been with Ellie for nine blissful years before the bolt-out-of-the-blue, before the 'I can't be with you anymore,' triggering tears from both and bewilderment from Ellie.

'What have I done wrong?' she pleaded, and he hung his head and admitted she had done nothing wrong.

'It's not you... it's me,' he lamely muttered.

'Is it a younger woman?' she asked, face blotchy and red, fists balled in anger. He choked back his response, shaking his head.

He *had* left it too long. And they were all younger – than him, anyway. That was inevitable when you were as old as Methuselah.

Seven years was just about right. Any longer and niggling doubts crept in. Comments about pictures in the attic turned from wry amusement to sullen fear as one of the pair put on a few pounds, found a few more grey hairs, a few new lines permanently etched on their face.

And the other? The other looked exactly the same as the day they'd met.

So, though it hurt – every *single* time – George knew to break up before the discrepancy between his claimed age and his looks morphed from 'lucky you!' to 'uncanny'. It was for the best, in the long run.

And George knew a lot about the long run.

Sometimes, he day-dreamed about the conversation he might one day have, if and when he could finally open up and tell the truth. Though he still didn't know exactly what the truth was. He thought of himself as immortal, and indeed, he hadn't aged these last 900 years, but only an infinity of time could ever prove his supposed immortality. Perhaps he just aged very, *very* slowly.

Many times slower than poor, distraught Ellie.

Sometimes, he wondered if it would be better to be caught cheating. To give her anger something tangible to focus on, to justify a 'good riddance!' as well as a 'goodbye'. But he couldn't bring himself to do it. That would be dishonest.

Sometimes, in the raw aftermath, he thought about never being in a relationship again. But George's 'never' was a bigger, scarier thing than a normal person's. And he knew the perfect balm for the hurt that he felt – that he caused – was to find new love.

And so, as the afternoon light began to fade, he took out his mobile. George was careful to stay up to date. Oh, he ignored the passing fads, the addictive and pointless games. But he'd had an smartphone even before he'd met Ellie and had upgraded as each new generation rolled out.

He knew the principles of Internet dating apps. Up until now, he'd had no need of them, but he was well aware that they had become the norm.

The day was virtually over by the time he'd set up his account and begun browsing, the park lights flickering on. His finger paused above the screen. He'd been swiping left, though not at an unseemly pace, letting each image soak into his consciousness and, as often as not, delving into the bio and any other photos before sadly dismissing the profile. The problem was one of memory: nearly everyone he saw reminded him of *someone*. Someone he'd once been close to. George had the best part of a millennium of baggage to avoid.

But the face that stopped his finger in its tracks did more than remind him. He half thought he recognised her.

Zahira: the profile name was unfamiliar, but there was definitely something about her. The face almond-shaped, the chin stronger than might be considered beautiful these days. Her skin was a warm, Mediterranean tone, eyebrows black and arched. Looks that wouldn't have been out of place on a bust of Queen Nefertiti–

And then he remembered. He'd seen her – or rather, someone who looked just like her – standing at the entrance to a recently opened tomb in the Valley of the Kings, while he'd been in the employ of John Gardner Wilkinson, one of the early British Egyptologists. The girl had fascinated him. Though he never heard her speak as she carried drinking water for the surveyors and she had, alas, vanished by the next day, he quickly twigged that she was far more knowledgeable than any of the native guides, most of whom seemed not to have left the bazaars of Luxor before.

The way she carelessly slopped her ladle, revealing the faint inscription on an overlooked stone. The way her lips moved as the archaeologist struggled to translate the hieroglyphs. The way she wandered to the top of a small rise, forcing an irate engineer to follow, his angry protest stillborn in his parched throat when he saw the evening shadows playing across the valley floor, the depressions there, and there, two more potential sites to investigate.

Ah, happy memories from another age! Funny how this Tinder picture brought it all flooding back. At least she didn't remind him of someone he'd once had a relationship with.

Idly, he read her bio. A curious girl, this Zahira; interested in the Classics, efficient and precise with her English while admitting it wasn't her first language.

George laughed. Nor, strictly, was English his. Or rather, not this English. An older one; only just beginning to absorb the words of the conquering Normans.

It would, he decided, be fun to find out what other memories this girl with the timeless looks sparked. Carefully, deliberately, he swiped right. Though there was every chance she would not reply. In his long lifetime, he had been rebuffed many times, the hurt inconsequential compared to that he had to go through every seven – or nine – years.

There was an echoing chime, from directly behind him, and he turned startled to see a woman holding her mobile phone.

'Hello George,' Zahira said, smiling at his shocked expression. 'Sorry. I'd already worked out there couldn't be many other Tinder users in the park at this time of night. It's probably very rude of me, but I've been waiting to see what you did next.'

For the first time since the Enlightenment, George found himself tongue-tied. The way she gently smiled, the way she held herself erect. This was not a girl who reminded of him of another, glimpsed for one surprising day two centuries earlier. This was that girl.

'Are you... immortal?' he asked, hardly daring to hope.

She reached out and took his hand, her skin warm and the touch... the touch was like coming home after a long journey.

'I'm not sure,' she laughed into the dusk. 'Ask me again. In a hundred years time.'

Crossroads

The devil was waiting at the crossroads.

'Howdy,' I said as I drew level. He was sat on a fence that looked too slight to hold him. Not that he was a big fella, he was kinda slim and about my height. Well dressed. His ancient face weathered and tanned.

He gave me a nod.

'Been here long?' I asked.

'Some,' he replied.

I dropped my kit bag to the scorched grass, before carefully lowering my guitar. We stood a while in mutual silence.

'Where you headin'?' he asked.

'Oh, I'm not particular,' I replied. 'Anywhere. 'Cept maybe back wheres I came from.'

He peered over my shoulder, looking across the prairie as if he could see the mess I'd left behind. He smiled and patted the black case by his side. 'Shall we play, to pass the time?'

'Sure,' I shrugged, and bent to the burlap bag I carried my guitar in. By the time I'd untangled the old thing he was sitting there, an ebony-black guitar slung over his narrow shoulders.

'Nice guitar,' I said.

He plucked a few strings, the mournful chords floating out into the early evening air. 'Thanks.'

I watched his fingers dance lightly over the strings, not a tune exactly, but not warming up neither. He drew to a halt. 'Seems 'bout right.' And then he looked back over at me.

I raised a knee, resting my boot on the bone-white fence, and lifted the battered instrument higher onto my lap. After the miles I'd already trekked that day, it was hardly a surprise there wasn't a string still in tune. I bent to my task, tweaking the keys, while he just sat there, his eyes closed until I was done.

'Your top string's still a touch low,' was all he said.

I gripped the nub of wood left where the peg had long since snapped off, fighting the tension in the string until I was sure I'd got it, feeling the blush fade. Then I defiantly lifted my head once more. 'Seems 'bout right,' I mimicked.

'Well now,' he drawled, amused. 'Perhaps you'd like a little sport. Something to make things more interesting.'

I stared at him. 'W-what do you have in mind?' I stammered, asking myself what my soul was worth, and what would I trade it for.

He looked at me long and hard, unblinking, until I dragged my gaze away. 'Your guitar,' he said, 'for mine.'

I laughed, feeling the sudden release of tension, and looked once again at the smooth black surface of his guitar, so dense and dark I could hardly see the grain of the wood, so dense I had to wonder if it were wood at all. 'What's in it for you?' I asked.

'Your guitar,' he repeated.

I frowned. 'But...'

'It's simple enough,' he said. 'If you can play better than me, then you deserve my guitar. And if you can't – well, we've passed some time, and nothing has really changed, has it?'

I couldn't see a downside and told him so.

He gave me a strange look that made me shiver, like winter had arrived just that moment. 'You'll see.'

I strummed my strings thoughtfully, looked to where he waited, wondering what he was waiting for. 'You first,' I said, and his face creased up once more into an easy grin.

And then he played.

He was good. That pitch-black guitar had a soulful resonance, a depth that even the wide open landscape couldn't dull. And his playing... he was real good. Heart-wrenchingly good.

When he was done, I gave the silence a respectful measure,

blinking moisture from my eye. 'Nice,' I said. 'Very nice.'

He said nothing, just tilted his head a little. Your turn, he was silently telling me.

'Course I already knew he'd won. But still, I wanted to play as well as I could. When you hear someone that good, that special, you want them to at least acknowledge you, to give you a nod of respect, of approval. Though, after a minute or so, thoughts of that and everything else drifted away on the soft prairie wind and I was just playing for the fun of it, like I always used to do.

Then my mind stumbled over thinkin' of the last time I'd played that particular tune, and who to, and what happened after, and that returned me with a sickening bump to the here and now. As the final chords jarred under my hesitant fingers I looked up at my audience of one, and gave him a smile. 'No need for a recount,' I said.

He shook his head, raised his thumb to his lips, the nail to the slim gap between his upper teeth. 'Don't be so hasty,' he said. 'Seems it ain't entirely fair, seems like you played well enough, but maybe that old guitar of yours ain't as good as you are. What say you we swap? And play one more round?'

Well I was keen enough. I'd been itchin' to get my hands on his guitar since I'd seen it. I shrugged nonchalantly. He lifted the sleek black instrument and, with a hand supporting the body and one on the neck, held it out to me.

Damn if it wasn't the heaviest guitar I'd ever hefted! I'd thought his two-handed grip was him just being extra careful and I paid him and it the same respect. Good thing to, as I would have near dropped it otherwise. Oh, it wasn't as heavy as a keg of beer, or a young heifer, or even Mary-Lou, all of which I'd hoisted in my time. But it was at least three times the weight of my cedarwood. Uncommon heavy for a guitar.

I balanced it carefully, feeling the coolness of its surface, easing its weight into a comfortable position. I gave its owner a wry grin, hardly knowing where to begin. Tried a few strings, then drew to a stop. The sound was clashing with itself, the tonewood kept the vibration going seemingly forever. I slowed it down, but it was still too fast, the noise an ugly jangle. Slowed it down once again, until it was almost a dirge, a lament, and the strings came alive under my fingers. It sure was hell to play, but the sound built and built, until it was almost playing itself.

When the final note was still slowly dyin', I looked around in surprise to see the stranger cinch tight the cord on my burlap bag. He nodded at me. 'Congratulations,' he said, and stood to go.

'Wait!' I cried out, confused. 'You're not going to play?'

He shook his head slowly. 'Nope. No point, I know when I'm beat. Enjoy your prize, and see ya around.'

I'd like to say there was a moment of dark premonition, as I watched him walk lightly away, his only baggage the guitar my older brother had left me, that day long ways back. But I'd be lyin'. Truth was, as I carefully laid the black guitar back in its jet black case, I could hardly believe my good fortune, hardly believe it was really mine.

I've been playing it ever since. Or maybe it has been playing me. Because since I picked up that guitar, I can't play no other. I can hardly bear the thought of letting it out my sight and even when I'm on the move, riding on the back of a pickup with the guitar safely in its case, I can still feel the smooth wood beneath my fingers, sense the taut strings, almost hear the notes I'll play as soon as we come to a stop.

It's bought me some success, sure. I make ends meet. I never want for a meal, or a drink, or a bed to lie in. The dark guitar on its own brings respect and I only have to strum a few bars to secure a gig, most anyplace I want to play. But not many places invite me back. The sound is so beguiling, so sorrowful, so sad, it ain't exactly what most joints want. But I can't play nothin' else. Damn guitar won't let me play nothing but the bleakest of blues, music to make grown men cry. Lost soul music. Music that, come the cold light of morning, casts a funereal pallor over the places I've played. So I have to keep moving, lugging my burden with me.

And the burden is a heavy one. 'Tain't just the weight, neither. It's the fear of damage, the fact I can't ever let no-one else play it, no matter who, and that distances me from my fellow musicians.

The girls want to touch it as well. The girls it, and my playing, attracts, and there's no shortage of them. But they're all damaged. Bad for me and I, bad for them. Another reason to keep movin'.

One day, maybe, I'll tear myself loose. Find a crossroads to sit at, wait for some wet behind the ears farm boy running from his past or seeking his fame, his fortune. I'll eye his lightweight, homespun, hand-me-down guitar with envy. And I'll offer him a trade: his guitar for mine, and head the way he came, to a simpler life, to somewhere I can settle down and finally stop running. Maybe find someone I can play my songs to, the songs I used to play, songs of friendship, of simple pleasures, of love.

Until then, I dance to the tune of this black as night, heavy as sin, demanding as the devil himself cursed guitar, and play on.

Kingdom

I've been counting the days and yet, when the light of the rising sun spills through the narrow cleft in the steep escarpment, as it does every year on this date, my stomach still twists itself into knots. I take one last look over my Kingdom – the single valley, bounded on three sides by mountains and on the fourth by a small lake that empties into a deep ravine – before hurriedly descending to the Great Hall to conduct the morning census and allocate the day's tasks.

I count twenty-three men, twelve women and two – no, *three* children. There used to be more. More men, more women, more children. My wife, the Queen, is not present. Some days she clings to my side, never more than a pace away from me. Today is not one of those days. Today, she is in bed, wracked with fear. She too has been marking the passage of time and though it grieves me to see her this way, I must leave her to battle her own demons, for I have much to do and little time to do it. I must prepare for our visitor.

The woodchopper's assistant is also not at the census. I check on him after lighting the fires in the kitchen. He's feverish and in his delirium he cries out in a guttural, foreign tongue. I dress his wound but there is little else I can do for him and the stench of decay foretells his doom. I wonder if there will be another brave enough to take his place?

It is at least a worry for another day, there is wood enough for the feast and I have given the woodchopper other duties.

Around noon the bell by the lake rings, a short, impatient peal and I carefully hand the sharp knife to one of the three cooks. King Ulfred, our neighbour in every direction and for many leagues beyond, is early. I quickly wash my hands and throw the fur-trimmed robe around my shoulders. By the time I swing open the heavy oak doors he is already there, skipping up the steps, lustily pulling on a rope.

'Nathaniel!' he cries. 'Greetings, old friend. I bring you new subjects.'

I mumble my thanks as he hands me the tether and the three men attached fall to their knees, cringing and forlorn. I rub the scarred tissue above my eye-patch. Two of them will not, I think, last to the next spring. The third, though his head is bowed, holds his shoulders erect despite the heavy pack he is carrying. The board around his neck proclaims him to be a counterfeiter. Very well, let us hope he is good with his hands.

King Ulfred claps me on the shoulder. He's beaming, his cheeks rosy from the row across the lake. 'A fine spring day! I should warn you, I've worked up quite an appetite. How fares the feast?'

Ulfred descends upon us each year at the spring equinox, when the ice has melted and the mountain lambs are young. He likes his lamb milk-fed; barely a month old. To my mind the meat is too lean and the cost to our small herd too high. But they are the King's favourite and so half a dozen of our precious lambs are crammed into the ovens and onto the spits. A glut of meat of which only the choicest will be offered to Ulfred.

'It is still being prepared, my liege. Perhaps some mutton stew while you wait?'

He screws up his face. 'I didn't come here for stew, Nathaniel! A refreshing goblet of water and then let us beat the bounds. We have much to discuss, fellow *King*.'

He gives me a narrow look and I silently berate myself for my careless slip. *My liege* is not how Kings refer to one another.

'Certainly, King Ulfred,' I say, pouring his drink. 'I'll just check on the kitchen.'

He downs the goblet and casts it aside. The still tethered prisoners cringe at the sudden noise it makes. 'Come now, I'm sure they can do without your ministrations for an hour. And I have need of your expert knowledge.'

We talk about his campaign in the South and his need to raise funds. I advise against the grain tax he proposes – last year's harvest was not a good one – and suggest a few alternatives. He harrumphs and says he'll think about it.

I fall silent. I was his advisor once; a trusted and loyal subject, my judgement valued. Until pride got the better of me and I began to think that my wisdom was such that I could do a better job than the King himself. My pitiful coup collapsed before it had even begun.

Too close to the court, I misjudged the level of fear that the King inspired outside of it. I know that fear now. I had thought my life forfeit; instead, it amused the King to banish me to this make-believe Kingdom along with my co-conspirators and our families, a lesson for others foolish enough to contest his might.

The day is warm and as we walk the thin trail that skirts the valley I slip the robe from my shoulders and carry it over my arm.

'Nathaniel,' King Ulfred tuts. 'Your shirt is threadbare and by the looks of the needlework you must have darned it yourself. Perhaps I should send you my tailor?'

I shrug, neither accepting nor rejecting his offer, wondering what the tailor has done to displease him. Perhaps no more than the ox Ulfred sent when I asked for help to plough the fields, the beast mewling in terror and bucking at the slightest touch. Had it done anything to justify being the butt of the King's cruel humour?

We pass the ruins of the stables. 'Improvements?' he asks, raising an eyebrow.

'A fire,' I reply simply.

'Any casualities?' He seems eager for the gruesome details.

I nod. 'Seven. It took hold too fast for them to escape. We... also lost the ox.'

A lie. The ox was dead long before the disaster that followed the first of the winter's snows.

'That *is* a shame.' King Ulfred shakes his head. 'They were fine stables. You will rebuild them, I hope.'

I look at him aghast. It was not a question. Was it an order?

He's holding my gaze, the smile frozen. 'Ah, yes. Now that the weather is better...' I fluster.

'Good! I do so enjoy our walks, Nathaniel. It is such a pleasure to be without my usual retinue, even if it is only for an hour, and it warms the heart to see what a fine King you have turned out to be. Long may you reign, hey?'

I shudder, a momentary weakness, but the King's back is turned and he fails to notice. We are at the rear of the hunting lodge that serves as my castle, near the kitchens, and the smell of roast meat fills the air.

'Ah, now I am truly ravenous,' he says, licking his lips. 'Let's eat!'

*

King Ulfred inhales deeply from the plate of tiny lamb chops. There is little to go with it: the last of the winter root vegetables, a few leeks, but he ignores these anyway. 'Exquisite!' he says as he pops a morsel of moist pink meat into his mouth. 'I'm really not sure the wine I have brought will do it justice.'

I eye the bottle enviously and he laughs and pushes it across the table. 'Here. For you and your lovely Queen.'

The Queen seizes hold of my hand, her grip fierce. I wait a moment, but she says nothing and as her grasp weakens I fill and pass her the goblet. She takes it eagerly, quickly draining the blood red liquor, a thin dribble escaping down her chin.

King Ulfred watches intently and calls for another bottle, but the Queen has slumped back into her seat and ignores the refill. Ulfred shrugs in disappointment and starts his feast in earnest. I sip my wine cautiously and watch him eat, remembering tales my wife once told me of exotic poisons the King employed to dispatch his enemies, catching them unawares during a feast such as this.

When he finally pushes back from the table, a satisfied look on his face, his plate is brimming with the slender white curves of stripped bones. 'I do believe I might have broken my record. Perhaps the Queen will do me the honour of counting?'

The Queen stiffens, clenching her jaw, and then after a long moment's pause she slowly reaches out to the plate I have placed in front of her and begins, her lips moving silently.

'Thirty-eight,' is all she says when she removes the last bone.

King Ulfred strokes his grease slicked beard. 'Thirty-eight eh? Two more than last year. My compliments to your cooks,' he says. 'And now, I have a gift for you.'

'A gift?' I echo in trepidation. The King's largesse is not to be trusted.

The King roots through the packs that were brought with him, pulling out a small parcel wrapped in white muslin.

I open it gingerly and then stare like a fool at the tiny embroidered tunic contained within.

'Fit for a Prince, no? And where is the little tyke?'

'Your Majesty,' I begin and then quickly stop.

'Come. You think I did not notice that the Queen was with child on my last visit?' King Ulfred waits until my head slowly dips in reluctant confirmation. 'So you have a child. A joyous occasion and one to be celebrated! A boy, I trust? Bring him to me.'

The Queen makes as though to stand, but I squeeze her thigh under the table and she shrinks back into her chair. I call for the woodchopper. The wait seems eternal before he enters, gently shielding the infant.

I stand and take the smiling babe from his scarred arms.

King Ulfred is at my side and quickly takes my burden from me, holding the small bundle aloft. 'A bonny child. And such beautiful eyes. His mother's, I believe?'

There's a quiet sob from the Queen and then Ulfred hands the child back. 'You're a lucky man, Nathaniel. You have what God in his infinite wisdom has denied me: an heir. Three wives, all young, one distinctly comely, and not a single blessed child.'

Ulfred reaches to his belt and pulls a dagger from its sheath, laying it down on the table next to his empty goblet. 'For a while, I thought I might groom a successor anyway. Some brilliant young man, plucked from obscurity, humbled by the unexpected honour, grateful for the opportunity. Not, as it turns out, one of my brightest ideas.'

I stare down at my feet, until I feel his grip on my shoulder and I slowly raise my head to look into his impassive face.

'As you know, Nathaniel, you owe me an eye. And I think it's time to collect, don't you? But I am not an unreasonable man. I will let you keep your sight if you offer me another's. Perhaps someone not yet tainted by your betrayal?'

*

The screams have finally stopped; the child has exhausted itself and sleeps fitfully. At long last the hall is silent, littered with the remains of the feast that none dare clean up.

I do not know where the Queen is, she wasn't to be seen when I returned from escorting Ulfred back to the lake. That was hours ago. Hours of pacing the slowly darkening hall, rocking my son back and forth as I held his tiny grasping hands away from the blood-stained bandage wrapped around his head.

How much can you be punished for one stupid mistake? And what if the sacrifice is not yours? What if it continues, year, after year, after year? Sometimes the sacrifice cannot be borne, and I dread what I might find when I seek out my wife.

When Ulfred next visits, shortly after the lambs are once more born, should I poison his meat in suicidal vengeance? Ah, but to what purpose, revenge? I could have wrestled the dagger from the King, or allowed him to take my sight, rather than that of my infant son. But what then? Who would look after him?

I shake my head, blinking the tear away. These are not options open to me. I have a duty to perform and though it rips my soul from me, it is not one I can shirk, I do not have the luxury of escape. My subjects, my wife, and my son – if he survives that long – they can choose for themselves whether they live or die.

But not I. For if I die, they die too: unsighted, they would not survive long without me. Thus am I destined to remain: the reluctant King in this, the land of the blind.

Stars

They fall from the sky and I must catch them.

I'm stepping off an Indonesian trawler, still tingling from the afterglow, when I feel the distant call. Somewhere in the Northern Hemisphere: Canada, perhaps. A journey of many steps.

It begins by mail van, ferry, and on foot. At the airport I'm disorientated by the sudden noise and chaos.

'How do I get to Canada?' I ask.

'You'll need to go via Singapore,' the girl behind the information desk says. 'Where exactly in Canada?'

By now the location of the fall should be on the tip of my tongue. But it isn't.

'I'm sorry,' I fluster, 'I'm not sure. Anywhere, I guess?'

She looks over my shoulder to a queue of less difficult passengers. 'Take a seat,' she gestures. 'I'm busy right now, but I'll see what I can do.'

On the metal bench, I hold my head in callused hands. The departures board shows mainly local destinations: Jakarta, Banda Aceh, Padang. Nothing resonates. My path is murky and confused, my thoughts fuzzy.

There's a touch on my arm – the girl from the information desk, holding a coffee and something even more welcome: a boarding card. 'I probably shouldn't be doing this, but you looked kind of lost. I've got you on a training flight as far as Frankfurt.'

I thank her profusely as she taps her watch. 'It's leaving now, otherwise I'd love to hear your story. Will you look me up when you come back this way?'

I tell her that if I can, I will, and I mean it, though I'm wary. People misinterpret the warm glow that lingers after a catch, expect more from me than I can give.

*

Lulled by the rumble of jet engines I dream of ripening maize, blue-tinged mountains on the horizon. But still no name comes. Have I been complacent? Is this a test of my faith?

In Frankfurt I thumb a tatty stack of foreign notes, wondering how far they'll get me.

'Welcome back, Mr Fletcher,' the guy working the ticket desk says with an easy smile. It's not my name. It's not even the name on the passport I just handed him and can only have been summoned by a computer glitch or data error, but as usual I go with the flow. Mr Fletcher is a regular traveller between Frankfurt and Calgary and has enough air miles to pay for an economy flight home.

But not the airport taxes. I'm directed to the bureau de change, where my wages from two months on a fishing trawler barely cover the departure fees.

Though I'm on my way I'm feeling rushed, agitated. As I tuck my canvas bag between my feet the Canadian across the aisle asks if this is my first flight.

I laugh and say no, and he smiles and says he still gets nervous as well. Tells me he's a farmer returning home after visiting his daughter. I ask him what he grows, and he says maize. Finally I can begin to relax.

*

But as he drives his pickup away from the airport I'm certain we're heading in the wrong direction. I crack and ask if he knows his way. He pulls over and, with the indicator tock-tock-tocking, he reaches across me and pushes the passenger-side door open.

'I'm headed East,' he says. '200 miles due East. I don't know where you're heading and I thought you didn't either, but you're welcome to find your own path.'

The first two cars are Calgary-bound and I wave them on into the thickening dusk, feeling precious time slip away. It's over an hour – an hour of listening to my heart beat too fast – before a truck with a farm feed logo fading on its side deigns to stop. The driver takes in my rough clothes, sturdy boots, and tattered bag and asks: 'Looking for work, son?'

I nod, uncertain, and he bangs twice on the panel behind. The tailgate swings down and a brace of strong arms haul me up.

It's dank and dark and the air is thick with tobacco and sweat. My hands twitch and flutter. I can feel the call; insistent, painfully so, and though I'm heading the right way, it's happening far too fast.

When the truck grinds to a halt I bolt into the cooling autumn night, laughter echoing as someone calls out: 'Don't piss on the corn!'

I plunge through the tall plants, knowing I'm too late. Will I find it lying on the dirt, soiled, damaged, the light bleeding away, testimony to my failure?

Bursting into the crop circle, I stop, astounded. A girl is stood in my place. I feel a tide of resentment, anger, and fear. For a moment I wonder if I can force from her what is rightfully mine. Then the envy slips easily away as she turns to me with arms spread wide and smiles the smile of a fresh catch and I'm bathed in her glow.

*

Afterwards, as we lie in the moonlight listening to the wind whisper through the maize, I realise I don't know her name.

'Stella,' she says, her naked belly rippling with silent laughter beneath my head. 'That's what my father called me: Stella.'

*

She returns a year later, just as the corn is ready to be harvested again. Dropping off her child – our child – with an impatient wave she tells me she's overdue in Wisconsin. As she steps to the side of a road a haulage truck pulls up and she gets in without a backwards glance.

*

I've settled here, doing a bit of this, a bit of that, but raising Oscar, mainly. He's four now and loves to hike. I have to carry him part way, otherwise we'd not get far, but he's always impatient to stomp the trails on his own. I think he likes it best when we set up tent and, as the fire dies down, he can stare into the vastness of the night sky.

I don't feel the pull of the stars anymore, but every so often I catch his eyes tracking something he can't possibly see. And then I know that this is borrowed time; that as soon as his little legs are strong enough, he'll be off.

The Black Bull

I desperately repeat my mantra as I walk slowly across the muddy field:

I must not run.

I must not fall.

And above all, the jet-black mountain of muscle and sinew that is busy snorting clouds of vapour-laden air and digging a mighty hoof through the soft earth, is not what it appears to be.

I'm further from the safety of the gate than from the beast when it finally breaks its stance and trots a few heavy paces towards me, expecting me to turn and flee. Instead, I take another tentative step and this time when it bows its head and launches forward it's the real thing: a thundering, full-blooded, earthshaking charge. My legs tremble and I stagger half a pace back before I can stop myself.

'I know what you are,' I say, in as steady a voice as I can manage.

It halves the distance between us in a single stride and my eyes clench shut as I fear my weeks of searching have misled me and it is exactly what it seems, which would make my mistake a very short-lived one indeed. I squint and realise it has pulled to a dead halt so close that I'm trapped between its horns, enveloped in a cloud of steamy breath.

There's a long pause before it speaks. 'You smell like him. Not a son, though. A grandson?'

'Nephew,' I reply, my heart still pounding.

'Ah yes. How is the old fool?' the bull asks.

It's talking about Uncle Mort.

*

Uncle Mort was supposed to be a safe, boring refuge from my

warring parents. I'd gone up for Trinity term at St Aidan's and by the time the summer holidays rolled around, I had no home to come back to. Dad had moved into his pied-à-terre in the city and Mum had closed up the family house to spend summer with her parents.

We sat in a pub garden – neutral territory – while they argued over who should have me. But it quickly turned into a slanging match over which was the worse parent and, as I slumped in my chair feeling rotten, I realised I didn't really want to spend time with either of them.

'Uncle Mortimer?' Mum said, surprised, when I told them of my decision. 'Are you sure, hon?'

I nodded, feeling the beginnings of tears, watching as both of them thought for a moment before scoring it a draw.

*

Uncle Mort lived in a ramshackle three-storey house on the rural outskirts of Bedford. He'd been a Professor of something or other at some time, but now... now I didn't know what he did, but it involved a lot of old books and very little else.

I don't think he'd had company for a while; he certainly didn't know what to do with me. He told me I had free run of the house and then, in the very next breath, he asked me to keep quiet while he was working, which was all of the time. He didn't have wi-fi, he didn't have Sky, and I was beginning to regret my choice when I came across the room in the basement.

It was locked, but the plate holding the padlock to the door jamb moved under my gentle push and it didn't take much wiggling to ease it from the rotten wood. Uncle Mort *had* said I had free run and, since his study was on the second floor, I knew I wouldn't be disturbing him, so I felt no guilt as I pushed the door open. I fumbled across the cold clammy plaster, looking for a light switch, before my fingers brushed the frayed end of a cord.

The bare bulb blinked alive. The room was full of shelves, each one crammed from top to bottom with dusty oil lamps, gleaming a dull yellow. At first, I thought they were miniature teapots, bronze maybe, with an unusually long spout. I picked one up. It was surprisingly heavy and as I turned it over I noticed strange shaped writing on the base. I was about to rub the dust off for a closer look when the firm grip of my uncle's hand on my shoulder made me jump in sudden fright.

*

The bull licks its lips. 'What do you want?' it asks.

'A wish,' I reply.

It snorts. 'You have no power over me, related or not. So what makes you think I will grant you one?'

I pause, trying to remember how I'd rehearsed this, but with the horns so close and those deep, dark, liquid eyes, I forgot the glib words I'd practiced.

'I know how to free you.'

*

Uncle Mort steered me out of the room, before trying unsuccessfully to secure the door. 'It's locked for a reason,' he said, his voice quavering. 'It's not safe to go in there.'

I shrugged. 'It's just full of old lamps–'

His hands came down again on my shoulders, gripping hard. 'Not just any old lamps,' he said. 'One of them is the lamp of a fiendish and powerful genie. The rest are identical copies, but all of them – all of them – are cursed.' He rocked back and forth on his heels. 'The inscription, in Aramaic of course, warns that anyone who rubs a lamp twice without making the genie within show the proper obeisance, will be forced to take the genie's place, for all time.'

He scratched his head, his eyes watering behind the thick and grubby lenses of his ancient glasses. 'I found the lamp on a dig in Palestine. When I rubbed it, another lamp popped into existence. And when I rubbed that one, another appeared! I tried to come up with a system for tracking them, making sure that I only ever rubbed the new lamp each time, when...'

Uncle Mort fixed me with a steely glance. 'Promise me you won't go back into that room?'

I looked up at his perspiring face, his eyes glittering in the dull light of the cellar. 'I promise,' I said. 'On my parents honour,' I added as an afterthought.

He sucked in a deep breath. 'When I reached three hundred and forty-three lamps, seven by seven by seven, a very magical number, it wasn't just a lamp that appeared; it was a full-grown and *extremely* angry bull.'

'It upset the shelves, sending the lamps I had so carefully arranged flying, and I barely got out unscathed. Of course, I couldn't work out which of the lamps was which anymore, which ones I'd rubbed already and which I had not, so I stacked them back up, and sealed the door.'

He rubbed the bridge of his nose. 'Thirty years I've spent trying to work out which lamp still has the genie inside – to no avail!'

If it had been anyone but my uncle telling it I would have thought it an odd joke. But, as far as I was aware, Uncle Mort didn't have a sense of humour. 'And the bull?'

Uncle Mort sighed. 'A magnificent beast. Pitch-black, powerful, massive; of ancient pedigree. I gave him to a local farmer, on the condition that he got him out of the cellar. He did exactly that, led him out as gentle as a lamb. Every time I see a black heifer around here I wonder if she's a child, or a great-grandchild, of that bull.'

*

The bull nods as I relate my uncle's story. 'I know all this,' it says. 'I was there.'

'But Uncle Mort didn't realise he'd released you, did he?' I point out. 'He thought you were just a trick, something to divert him from the genie that was in one of the lamps. Uncle Mort said you went quietly?'

The bull shifts its head gently from side to side. 'He wished it so, in the strongest possible terms.'

'Why stay a bull?' I ask.

The bull jerks its head, its lips curling in distaste. 'Because if he knew I was the genie he'd order me around. I'd be his slave.'

'But you don't want to be a bull forever?' I say.

'Why not?' it replies. 'It's not a bad life. I've been through three owners already. No one knows exactly how old I am. And that doesn't even require any magic, just plain old-fashioned greed. Each farmer who sells me lies about my age to maximise his returns. Speaking of age, how old is your uncle now?'

I stare at the bull. It looks to be in its prime, but then, it probably did the day it emerged in Uncle Mort's cellar. Was it waiting patiently for the death of my uncle to secure its freedom?

'Oh, he's in fine form. Fit as a fiddle. We come from quite long-lived stock ourselves, you know.'

The bull harrumphs. 'So, brave little man, talk. How do I secure my freedom?'

I told him.

'Can't be done,' the bull says after a moment's thought. 'The curse cannot be removed from the lamp.'

I scratch my head, momentarily defeated. 'But you could collapse all the lamps back into one? And make uncursed copies?'

The great black head dips slowly. 'That, I can do.'

*

I climb the steps to my uncle's office with trepidation. Tapping lightly on the door I don't wait for a response before I push it open with my foot and rub rigorously at the lamp in my hands. Uncle Mort yells incoherently and leaps up from his desk.

'What are you doing? What have you done?' He stares at me in horror.

'That,' I say, 'was the last of the three hundred and forty-three lamps. I've rubbed every single one and there's no genie in any of them.'

He rocks back on his feet, his mouth a perfect O.

'And there's something else,' I raise the lamp and quickly rub it again.

'Noooo...' his shout tails off as I breathe on the now shiny surface and gave it one last polish with my sleeve.

'There,' I say triumphantly. 'No genie, and no curse.'

'But the bull... the lamp... the three hundred and forty-three lamps!'

I shrug. 'Old magic, perhaps. But not active anymore.'

Uncle Mort leans on his desk for support and waves a trembling hand at the piles of discarded parchment scattered across every surface. 'Thirty years, all for naught! I wish I'd never found that blasted lamp! What do I do now?'

I think for a moment. 'Go back to the Middle East, dig up something new. Or teach. Or, heck, buy a yacht and live a life of idle luxury. With a cellar full of solid gold lamps, I *think* you can do anything you want, Uncle.'

*

I drag the memo-recorder out of my pocket and hit play. 'I wish I'd never found that blasted lamp!' the tinny voice echoes.

The bull nods. 'Not exactly admissible in a court of law, but it's enough. You've fulfilled your end of the bargain. So, what is your wish? Do you want your parents back together?'

'Would that make them happy?' I ask, already knowing the answer.

I reach into my satchel, delicately removing the lamp, the original lamp, the one still inscribed with the curse.

The bull's eyes flash red and it lowers its horns towards me. 'Be careful, little man!'

'It isn't what you think,' I say, gathering my thoughts.

My uncle had freely given me the lamp, not knowing it was any different from the other three hundred and forty-two copies, but still, I wasn't the genie's master unless I wished him back into it. Made him show the proper obeisance, as my uncle had put it.

And I'd considered doing exactly that, briefly, until I'd thought about Uncle Mort's thirty wasted years. We all daydream of having a genie at our beck and call, but when it actually happens, when you hold that lamp in your hands... Maybe in the end, I lacked the imagination.

'I wish,' I begin, as the bull's eyes narrow and its body tenses, 'I wish for you to put this lamp somewhere safe, where it can never be found, never be rubbed.'

The bull breathes out slowly and then it nods, and the lamp vanishes from my hands, leaving nothing but an odd tingle and the memory of its weight.

'It is done. Neither man nor beast will ever find it. And I thank you. It is the one wish which not only frees me but means I will stay free.'

I smile and stand there, waiting patiently.

The bull taps its hoof. 'There was something more?'

'I was waiting for you to turn back into a genie. I'd like to see that.'

The bull sways its head, suddenly vague, its eyes darting away from mine. 'Oh...there's no rush.'

The penny drops. 'You're...you are *actually* a bull, aren't you?' I ask in amazement. 'But the magic? The talking?'

The bull solemnly nods. 'I don't know whether I ended up inside the lamp by accident or by design. I was merely a simple beast when first I was trapped. But after two thousand years inside a magic lamp, some of the power rubs off.

'So yes, I am a bull, and I am a genie. Though with the lamp far away, my powers will slowly fade and I will become again what I always was: a bull. Now though, it's time for you to leave. There's a rather perplexed farmer watching us from the north gate.'

'What will you do? Where will you go?' I ask. There are so many questions, so much I still want to know.

'Go? Do?' the bull snorts. 'These are not concerns for me, I am a bull. Nor as it happens, are they concerns for you. No, your concern, brave little man, solver of puzzles, liberator of genies, is how much of a head start I'm going to give you.

'Now, RUN!'

Worming Advice For Werewolves

If you have a werewolf in the family as we do, then you'll already know how boisterous these adorable beasts can be. You'll know all about the need to safely secure your loved ones (or perhaps yourselves!) whenever the full moon comes around, plus the nights either side, just in case.

But have you stopped to think about your lycanthrope's digestive health?

Households with vampires, to some degree, have it easy. While there are those, this columnist included, who find the undead cold, even aloof, there can be no denying that they are much easier to look after, requiring only such simple expedients as clearly defined zones into which they are not invited. Zones which can easily be reinforced with the liberal application of garlic. And the same rings true for their health: vampires are fussy eaters, or should I say drinkers, and this means that they suffer from remarkably few parasites and digestive complaints.

Werewolves are another matter entirely.

While there are some health issues that you can only hope and pray to avoid, such as the fortunately rare Variant Creutzfeldt-Jakob disease, there are others which are alas exceedingly common. Tapeworms, threadworms, roundworm, even whipworm. All acquired by the eating of uncooked meat.

Expecting your werewolf to fire up a barbecue or to use a meat thermometer while in their turned state isn't exactly practical, so it's essential that you keep up to date with their worming treatment, available from your local pharmacy.

Because rest assured, however healthy he or she looks, your werewolf, if left untreated, has worms.

A note on when best to give your werewolf their medication. I really shouldn't have to say this, but it is neither necessary, nor indeed prudent, to attempt to give de-worming pills during a full moon. Your werewolf will suffer from worms the whole month round, not just while turned. In our household, we give the treatment the day of the new moon. This is completely safe, very easy to remember, and any worm eggs or larvae they might have picked up in the last lunar cycle will by then be in a treatable, non-dormant state.

If your lycan is embarrassed about their wild behaviour, possibly even in denial about 'that time of the month', it may be necessary to slip their medication unawares into their food. A curry or hearty stew should do the trick, though do make sure they wolf it all down.

Finally, it is sensible to be aware of the health hazards of worms and other disease vectors for non-lycan family members. These are, after all, by and large human parasites, so it is wise to be scrupulously hygienic when cleaning up after your werewolf as the night fades and they come back to you, tail between their legs. Non-rip garbage bags, disposable gloves and the strongest disinfectants are advised for cleaning up any blood or meat fragments, while mouthwash and dental floss will help with their oral hygiene. Though once again this is best left until morning light.

If you take these simple precautions, then you can sleep soundly behind thick iron bars as your relatives heed the call of the moon, safe in the knowledge that you have done your very best to keep them healthy and happy.

The Sword Master

The Town Bully returned home from the wars. In his absence the town had grown too small somehow and so he set out once again, seeking word of the legendary Sword Master, that he might hone his skills.

No-one he met seemed able or willing to tell him the way, until at long last a nervous woodsman directed him northwards. Though the route led into the mountains and over terrible passes, the Town Bully knew it would be worth it. Once he had learnt all there was to know, what riches, what fame would lie in his grasp!

As he left the farthest reaches of the Kingdom, the woodsman watched him go, turned and spat. 'Good riddance.'

His wife looked up at him with concern. 'You don't worry he'll be back?'

The woodsman laughed. 'He will find the path peters out and becomes merely a track the goats use. May the mountain take him, the evil brute!'

*

The Evil Brute struggled on through the cold winter, not knowing to despair, not knowing to hold any strength in reserve, and whether it was this, the surprisingly noble lineage of his horse, or simply that the mountain gods wanted him no more than the towns he'd passed so malevolently through, history does not relate. He survived.

Coming down the other side of the mountain range he found himself in a different, harsher Kingdom, where the people were harder than those he'd left behind. He took one look at the group of men who greeted him with dark sullen glances, swallowed his usual threats and demands, and asked, as politely as he knew how, where to find the Sword Master.

They laughed at him and the Evil Brute bristled, his hand flying to his sword just as a young man stepped through the crowd.

'Stranger, pay my friends no heed. They are merely amused to find that you have come such a long way, over impassable mountains, to speak to our Sword Master.'

The crowd laughed again and the youth mock-frowned. 'You will find him just beyond the ford on the road out of town.'

*

The Stranger shrugged and tipped his hat. As he trotted away the laughs erupted anew and he looked over his shoulder to see them heartily clapping the back of the youth who had spoken.

He vowed that once he been to see the Sword Master, he would return and teach these men a lesson in respect.

He almost rode past the cottage in the evening gloom. True, it was just after the ford and he could see no other houses that side of the mountain stream, but still, it was little more than a two-roomed shack. An old man was tending the garden and the Stranger thought that at least he would know how much further he must ride.

He vaulted off the horse to land lightly by the old man's side. 'Old man, do you know where the Sword Master lives?' he asked.

The man looked up, his weathered face betraying no signs of emotion. Just my luck, thought the Stranger, a simpleton.

The old man's glance took in the hoof prints churning up the bed of delicate spring vegetables and the lamb's lettuce trampled beneath the Stranger's fancy boots.

'What do you want with him?' he asked coldly.

The Stranger almost damned the old man for his impertinence, but something about the way he held the hoe in his gnarled hands gave him pause.

'I am here to learn,' he said simply.

'I am the Sword Master!' the old man thundered. 'And you are on my land – draw your sword!'

The Stranger drew, eagerly, swiftly, and just as swiftly the old man turned his back and pottered towards the little cottage, calling out as he went, 'You are not ready to learn.'

The Stranger was devastated. He had come all this way, only to be dismissed so casually. At first he thought it must be a mistake, the old man was no Sword Master, just a peasant aggrieved that the Stranger's horse had nibbled on a few measly shoots.

But as he rode on, looking for the true Sword Master, everyone he asked directed him back to the miserable cottage by the ford, only now he knew why they laughed. They laughed at him, they laughed because he was a failure.

What had he done wrong? All the Sword Master had seen him do was to draw his sword. Perhaps that was it? Perhaps he had to show that he was worthy even in that simple act?

*

The Failure set to practising. He practised how to draw his sword swiftly. He practised how to draw his sword silently. He practised drawing his sword when the scabbard was on a table, or beneath a bed, or hard against a tree.

And soon enough, he got to practise it for real. This Kingdom was less forgiving than the one he had travelled from. They bristled at the slightest offence and while his draw was indeed quick – much quicker than theirs, the Failure noted with satisfaction – they travelled in packs and fought as one.

Disarmed and beaten, his boots and other belongings were taken from him, leaving only his sword and his horse.

He rode after them, fury in his heart, and was soundly beaten once more for his troubles. He knew then why they had left him sword and horse. For the *sport*.

Realisation was slow, as it battled with his twice-wounded pride. To draw a sword was not an action that could be undone. To draw it first when outnumbered, was the act of a fool.

He also realised that a Sword Master in this nation of swordsmen was indeed a figure to be respected. He *must* make him train him!

*

The Fool returned to the little cottage by the stream. He tethered his horse and stood at the gate of the garden. It was summer and the vegetables were growing large and healthy even in this rocky, shaded land.

He called out to the old man weeding the rows: 'Sword Master! May I enter?'

The Sword Master stood slowly, stretching his back and holding aloft the stick he had been leaning on. 'Draw your sword!' he barked, suddenly light on his feet.

The Fool's hand twitched and then he raised it clear of his pommel. 'Sir, with respect, I am not here to fight, I am here to learn.'

The old man lowered his stick and nodded. 'Come.'

Inside the cottage the Fool was surprised and delighted to see dozens of swords hanging on the bare walls. Truly then, this was the Sword Master.

He wondered idly if these had all been won in battle – the spoils of victory – or were they given as rewards by the noblemen the Sword Master had fought for? Or perhaps, less prosaically, the Sword Master was simply a collector of swords.

The old man watched the smile grow on the Fool's face and then he demanded: 'Choose your weapon.'

This stumped the Fool. So many to pick from! There were huge double-handed swords he doubted he could even lift, curved scimitars from exotic lands, thin gleaming rapiers...

His eyes alighted on a sword the elegance of which he had never seen before, it shone brighter than the rest, a sword fit for a Prince. 'That one,' he said, 'the one with the strange lettering.'

The old man took it gently from the wall. 'Ah yes. Finest steel. A keen edge and well balanced. But, I'm sorry, you are not ready to learn.'

The Fool stood there for a moment in total shock. Again, to come this far and to fail at the first hurdle! He bowed his head in shame and quietly left.

He thought long and hard about what his mistake had been. Had not the Sword Master said it was a fine weapon? Perhaps it was too like his own? His sword, it was true, was not inlaid with silver and lacked the beautiful filigree on the handle, but did that matter?

Oh what a naive idiot he'd been! To the Sword Master, it was obvious he had chosen his own weapon in prettier form!

*

But then, which *was* the right choice? Perhaps there wasn't one, thought the Naive Idiot. Perhaps he needed to be proficient in all of them.

As a travelling mercenary, he could not carry more than a couple of blades, but whenever he could he would beg to borrow the swords of others. He practiced with hand-and-a-half swords, short swords, daggers, even axes and spears. He was almost swayed by the delicate curve of an oriental blade, but in the end none were quite as comfortable to him as the dull grey metal he had had since his first battle, scratched and pockmarked as it was.

The Naive Idiot sat bolt upright. Oh, truly he a dolt! It was obvious now: the weapon he should have chosen was the one that had been strapped to his waist. However able he was with any other blades, none were quite so accustomed to his hand as that he had carried for so many years, the one that fitted him like a glove, that had been tested in battle and held no surprises, no unknowns.

*

The Dolt returned to the cottage by the river. A full year had passed, but once again the garden was blooming and again the old man welcomed him into the house and bade him choose his weapon.

The Dolt patted the trusty steel at his side. 'Master, I can fight with any of these, but I choose the sword I am already carrying.'

The old man nodded. 'Bold words, impetuous youth. And with these weapons that you can wield, how many men have you slain?'

*

The Impetuous Youth, though he did not feel much like a youth anymore and hadn't for some time, felt warmth at the Sword Master's words and his chest swelled. At last, the old man recognised his worth.

'Dozens, Sword Master!' he boasted. 'Just last month, I was in a battle against three of Lord Qi's best men. I slew two and mortally wounded the third.'

The old man's face was cold and the Impetuous Youth felt the hairs on the back of his neck rise as the Sword Master turned away and once again he heard him say, 'You are not ready to learn.'

It nearly crushed him. Failure once again! How many was he supposed to have slain? How many defeated foes would make him a worthy student?

He returned to his nomadic life, with death a constant companion. The notches on the belt of his scabbard threatened to eat their way through it. He stopped keeping count.

Hired to tackle a notorious gang of footpads on a busy road between two towns, he descended upon them like a whirlwind. But they were no more the dangerous cut-throats he'd been warned against than he'd been when first he'd entered their country. They were merely cold, hungry youths and quickly surrendered their arms, frightened for their lives. They recognised him and his sword, they knew his reputation as a notorious blackguard and that terrified them even more.

Their fear and the thought of bloodshed sickened him. He took their weapons, gave the ring-leader a hard paddle on the backside, and told them that they were all idiots who would surely fall foul of the next person they tried to rob who knew how to handle a blade.

*

From that day, the Blackguard practised to disarm. True, that occasionally meant the cutting of a weapon-bearing limb, or the use of his pommel on the back of some opponent's head, but he killed only when he had to.

It was more challenging to do so and his services were somewhat less in demand as a result. This suited the Blackguard well: he had more time to think, more time to read.

He became a respected tactician. He worked out ways to win battles decisively: morale-sapping routs that would force the enemy to surrender in short order.

*

The Tactician trained the men he commanded to sweep through those arrayed against them, nicking here, slicing there, not getting bogged down by the tiresome business of hacking their opponents to death.

'Keep moving,' he advised, 'and the target will not be you.'

After yet another successful battle, the commanding General congratulated him with a wry grin.

'I'm glad you're on my side,' he said. 'I dare say there's no man alive who can teach you anything about the art of war.'

At that moment, the Tactician knew that the General was wrong: that there was something he still had to do.

The garden was in a state. Weeds grew rampant. Part of the fence was down and something – a deer perhaps – had got in and devoured half the crops.

The Tactician was shocked. He called for the Sword Master, but there was no response. A thin, feeble wisp of smoke rose from the cottage chimney and he went to the door, careful not to tread on the few remaining cabbages.

He thought at first that the cottage was empty: the fire was little more than glowing embers, not enough to chase away the chill of the mountain's shadow. Then a bundle of blankets stirred and coughed in the corner.

The Tactician leapt to the Sword Master's side.

'Water...' the old man croaked, and the Tactician quickly took a bucket to the icy stream. Coming back, he grabbed a couple of logs for the fire. After giving the Sword Master a small drink he pulled the cup away from him.

'Not too much,' the Tactician warned. 'I'll make soup.'

The Sword Master took a long time to get better. The Tactician weeded the garden and harvested what crops he unearthed, but as winter approached he knew it would not be enough.

He rode into town and sold his medals and battle trinkets for dried meat and rice. He was bristling with fury. 'How can a whole town stand by while an old man starves to death!' he demanded.

The store owner shrugged and in that expression the Tactician recognised the youth who had given him directions the first time he'd ridden through the town, many years before.

'This is a border town. Life is hard here. A Samaritan who gives to another will not have enough for himself.'

*

When he returned to the cottage the Samaritan was dismayed to see the Sword Master curled up by the fire, but still shivering as though lying in snow. He gathered him up, amazed at how light he'd become, and wrapped him in the blankets, trying to rub the cold flesh back to life.

'Stop, please,' the Sword Master murmured. 'You have been kind, but that hurts and disturbs my thoughts. I wish to die in peace.'

The Samaritan stumbled over his words. 'You can't die, you have so much to teach me!'

The Sword Master smiled and beckoned the Samaritan closer, gripping his hand.

'Dear friend, I have taught you everything I know,' whispered the old man as his grip weakened and his hand went limp.

*

The Dear Friend buried the old man under the shade of an apple tree close to the stream. He stared into space for a while, as small birds pecked at the freshly turned earth, and then he took up the hoe to tend the neglected garden.

But his sword kept getting in the way, so he went into the silent cottage and, finding a couple of nails, hammered them firmly into the wall.

*

And there, amongst the many others, the Sword Master hung up his sword.

Penny Prince

A faint ringing of metal on metal, the *tink!* of a coin glancing against a stone wall, a pause before the soft, final landing, and the day's work begins anew. I briefly consider ignoring the summons, as I do every dank, dark morning, but the memory of my mother's words chide me from my nest of leaves and moss.

I push myself to my hands and knees and feel something squelch under my palm. I gather the meaty worm to my lips, grateful for the nourishment, before crawling to where the coins come to rest.

Digging with my fingertips through the loose dirt, I glance with squinted eyes at the bright, diced disk at the top of the well. The sky is blue, today; but it'll be a while before the unseen sun spills enough light to cut the subterranean gloom, before the metal grid casts its latticed shadow on the glazed bricks high above.

I find the offering, a penny. A hopeful sign that a good day is ahead of me. I pop it into my cheek for safe keeping, sucking on its brassy coldness while I wait to see if any more coins are forthcoming.

There's nothing. No movement, no sound, no voices. I suspect the penny was an early morning offering from someone who didn't even break step in passing.

I thread my way back to where my mother silently waits, presenting her with the first coin of the day. I take her hand, place the coin in it, and feel it slip between the cold, hard fingers. Were I so minded, I could count the pile that has grown up over time, to know how long it has been since she last moved, last spoke, last closed her fingers around a coin.

In the days when the pile was only a dozen strong she must still have been proud of me, for those days were bountiful; the small alcove in which she sits writhed with insects and I did not go hungry. But that time is long gone, the coins now threaten to spill from her lap into the tunnel and only the occasional ghost-white millipede crawls over her thin limbs and gaping ribs.

I pace out my territory: the three tunnels with their neat alcoves, each for a different type of coin. Then on to the dank ledge that overlooks the storm sewer where I relieve myself. Once I have done my rounds I settle into a nook by the shaft and idly pick through the leaf litter for woodlice and other morsels, while I await the next of the day's offerings.

*

My mother did not call the coins *coins*, nor did she call them *offerings*. She called them *wishes*.

'What sort of wishes?' I asked.

Each coin, she said, held a person's secret desires, which is why they were precious, why we must carefully look after them.

'What sort of desires?'

'Oh, all kinds,' she said. 'Money, love, health. Serious things, frivolous things. Escape...'

I shook my head. Why would you wish for money while throwing it away?

'What happens to the wishes, mama?'

She gave me a look, of sorrow, of pity. 'Sometimes, just wishing is enough, a desire to change is enough. Sometimes, the wishes are forgot almost as soon as the coin leaves the hand. And sometimes... sometimes the most foolish wishes of all are granted.'

*

My mother had the knack of knowing what coin had been thrown from on high, by the noise it made as it bounced off the iron grill or against the moss-covered walls. 'A tuppeny wish', she would say, or 'a ten-penny wish'.

Little surprise the first word I ever spoke was 'penny'.

*

When I was older and she less able or less willing to crawl back and forth, I would gather the coins for her, bringing them back to be sorted and neatly stacked, as I still do today, in the alcoves that honeycomb the tunnels below.

She taught me to recognise the coins by touch. By the light of the blue sky, or on the rarest of summer nights, by that of a full moon, she told me tales about what I could dimly see, the ten pence piece with its lion proudly wearing a crown, or the perennial penny and its chained metal grid, so like the one that sits at the top of our well, that divides the high from the low. She said it was a 'portcullis'.

*

'My prince', my mother called me. 'My penny prince.'

*

Except for that one time, when she caught me trying to climb the shaft, trying to reach the distant portcullis. I made it as far as the last five feet; there the glazed bricks shone in the harsh, bright sunlight and offered me no purchase; too smooth to grip, not crumbling like those below. I stayed there a while, wondering how I could bridge the impossible gap, until my mother found me.

She slapped me, called me 'god-forsaken', and then burst into tears, telling me she did it out of worry, out of fear; that no good would come to either of us from up there.

I cried that I wasn't trying to get 'up there', that I just wanted to see what lay beyond. She hissed, 'If you can see them, then *they* can see you!'

I knew this wasn't true. I'd seen the sun-lit faces staring down into the black depths in which I was hidden. I'd watched them with longing, not knowing what it was I yearned for. But I said nothing, still shocked from the sharp retort of my mother's hand against my cheek.

*

82

She told me that up there, in the place that the coins came from, each coin had a different value. She taught me to recognise the numbers on the coins. 'A pound is worth a hundred pennies,' she would say.

I was curious. 'Is a pound wish worth a hundred penny wishes?'

'No,' she said, with fierce passion, 'Wishes are special to the person who makes them and we must look after them all, make sure none are ever lost. This is our duty, yours and mine. The value of the coin itself doesn't matter. Except...' she trailed off.

'Except?' I prompted.

She sighed and I felt the breath of warm air in the cool, damp tunnel. 'A silver sixpence.'

I could not recall ever having seen a sixpence coin.

'I had a sixpence once, a proper one, a silver one.' she murmured, in the dreamy voice in which she sometimes told her tales.

'Where is it?' I asked.

'Lost,' she said. 'Or transformed. I don't know. I threw it into the well.'

I rocked back on my heels. 'You threw a coin into a well – *this* well?'

'Yes,' she said.

I slipped away, to sit and think. When I returned, she was waiting for me as if our earlier conversation had not ended. Which, I suppose, it hadn't.

'What's it like?' I asked, 'Up high? Is it like the stories you tell? Are there really Princes and Princesses? Lions and feather crowns and magic?'

She smiled, a weary smile, a smile that seemed to say that she had known this day would come.

'No, not quite. But nor is it like anything down here,' she said. 'It is much, much larger. There are trees and buildings, buildings as tall as this well is deep, taller even. You can see the sun, feel it on your skin, and there are oh so many people.'

'More than a hundred?' I asked, in disbelief.

'Many more,' she laughed. 'Men, women and children. Animals too: dogs, and cats, and foxes.'

How crowded it must be, I thought. And I wondered how those fabled beasts compared to the mice and the occasional dead rat that floated by in the storm-sewer that bordered our domain.

'What did you wish for, mama?' I asked.

She gripped my hand, gripped it so tightly that it hurt and gripped even harder as I tried to pull away. 'Never, *ever,* tell anyone what you wish for. You hear me? *Never.*'

*

I pieced it together as best I could. It had something to do with me, though when she made her wish I had not yet been born. It had a lot to do with her family, about whom she rarely spoke. And it had something to do with falling. 'I am a fallen woman,' she would say, with a little laugh that sometimes turned into a sob.

I didn't understand. How could she have fallen, when the grid at the top of the well only let coins and leaves pass? What could she have wished for that might cause the earth to swallow her up, the portcullis closing behind her, an impassable barrier between what she once knew and where she lived now?

*

Sometimes the size and the shape of the coin are familiar, but the design less so. They change with the year, the year with which they are etched, the numbers that slowly march onwards. A new coin gleams in a way its older companions do not, but there is no-one to tell me its story.

Sometimes, a particular coin is thrown no more, or only very rarely. And sometimes the coins are strange, I cannot understand their markings. They bear neither King nor Queen, and I wonder who it is they expect will grant their wishes?

*

I wake once again to the faint sound of a coin against stone. Has the day begun so soon? But when I crawl to the shaft and stare upwards, it is the moon that I see, the full moon, hanging dead centre and imprisoned.

There is a chill to the air and I listen for noise; for the giggles, the laughter, for the other strange sounds that sometimes accompany such night offerings. There is the only the soft sigh of the wind and the mournful hoot of the unseen beast my mother called an 'owl'.

My fingers feel their way across the damp ground, ignoring the woodlice and the snails that I would normally linger over. At last, I run my fingers across the coin and I hold it to the light of the moon above.

I tremble in the cold night air. It is a silver coin of unfamiliar size, lighter even than a penny, and it bears a King's head instead of one of the four Queens; the girl, wreathed by leaves; the young woman, the crown borne proudly high upon her head; the mother, her shoulders draped in cloth; or the aged Queen that only appeared after my mother had tucked herself into her alcove and stopped naming the coins as they fell, the coins that continued to change their year and design, ignoring her silence.

Gently I rub the dirt from the reverse, read the words that appear there. 'Sixpence' it says, as a shiver runs down my naked spine.

My mother had a sixpence once. She wished upon it, though she would never tell me what she wished for. Whatever it was, it allowed her to pass through the solid metal barrier at the top of the well and she'd regretted it ever since.

'Be careful what you wish for,' she'd said.

Is this my mother's sixpence? I could give it back to her. Would she take it? Or would it too slip through her still, fleshless fingers?

With the moon so full and so perfectly centred, this is a

magical moment and perhaps the coin, and therefore the wish, are meant for me.

I close my eyes, mutter my words and lightly throw the shiny sixpence.

I do not hear it hit the ground.

When I peek through slitted eyelids there it is: floating before me, sparkling in the moonlight, slowly spinning as it rises up and up, back through the portcullis, towards the black clouds that have begun to threaten the moon.

I wonder where it is going. And whether my wish will still be granted.

The first heavy drops of rain fall onto my upturned face moments later.

'Be careful what you wish for.' My mother's last words echo in my mind.

My mother never liked storms. She'd always been nervous, crouched on the ledge above the sewer, watching anxiously as the levels rose. Worried, I think, that the black, turgid waters might spill into our tunnels. They never had. This had always been a dry well.

But then, it had never rained like this before. As the ground beneath my feet turns to mud, as that mud creeps up my ankles, to my thighs, to my knees, as I hear and feel the thunder crack above and the angry noise of the gushing sewer below, my breath rasps and my heart thuds.

'Mother,' I whimper, but I know now that she cannot answer, will never again answer.

I had wished to be borne up, to be lifted to the portcullis, so that I might finally see what lay beyond.

The water surges, cold and rank. I had not specified by what.

Desperate fingers clawing at the crumbling walls, I begin my climb.

Miscellaneous, Spooky, Weird

'Emergency. Which service?'

This is what you'll hear if you are unfortunate enough to need to call 999.

There are, of course, many more than three options.

The AA – the car breakdown company, not Alcoholics Anonymous – once claimed it was the Nation's 4th Emergency Service. But that was just self-serving, aggrandising claptrap.

After Police, Fire, and Ambulance, come other services you might know to ask for by name: the Coast Guards, Mountain Rescue, Bomb Disposal and the like. And then there are those you probably won't; it is the dispatch operator's job to forward you on to the appropriate people, working from a list which is rather longer than you would suppose.

There are departments that the Government, Freedom of Information Act or not, will point-blank deny exist, until that one time they are needed. Some are the stuff of nightmares: cures as terrible as the disease, only to be contacted in the direst of apocalyptic emergencies.

At the very bottom of the list, there's Mavis Ethelwright. Not by name, she's listed as: "Miscellaneous, Spooky, Weird", but from Land's End to John o' Groats, there is only one phone that will ring if that call is made and it stands on a lace doily on a small occasional table in a semi-detached on the edges of Walthamstow. There is a reason she lives there and a reason so much of the Hackney Marshes will never be built on and the two might be connected, but that is for another story.

Mavis was in her favourite armchair when the red Bakelite telephone rang. It rang seven times – just long enough for her to finish her cup of tea – before she reached out and picked up the handset.

'Yes, dear?' she answered.

'Um, is that...?' the emergency dispatcher warbled.

'This is Mavis Ethelwright.'

'Ah. I think I have the wrong–'

'Oh, I don't think so, dear,' Mavis said, peering at the leaves at the bottom of her teacup. 'I don't think you have the wrong number at all.'

Miscellaneous, Spooky, Weird does not have official transportation, so after taking the particulars from the still wary Dispatch, Mavis rang for a taxi. Miscellaneous, Spooky, Weird does not, as a general rule, require immediate response; sometime before the next Tuesday is what appears on her rather reluctantly filled-in Service Level Agreement.

She gathered her things and, after performing a quick ward to protect her home, she went out the front and sat on the small garden bench to wait for her ride.

'Alwight, Mavis?' the taxi driver said as he drew up.

'Oh yes, thank you, Alan.'

Alan hopped out of the cab and swung open the back door.

'The front, I think, Alan,' she said.

He drew in a sharp breath. 'That serious?'

'I'm afraid so,' Mavis said. 'I'll be wanting to see where we're going.'

'Right-ho.' He wasted no further time, nearly breaking into a run as he rounded the taxi and retook his seat. 'Where to?'

'South,' Mavis said, squinting at an old iron nail dangling from a piece of yarn.

Mavis Ethelwright is England's only official witch. That England's other witches tend to keep a rather lower profile has a lot to do with the oldest on that list of emergency services, a hangover from the sixteenth century and never fully disbanded. Mavis calls them the *Drown 'em and Burn 'em Brigade* and a number of her spells and incantations have more to do with protecting herself from them than the evil power that lurks deep in the marshes.

Their destination became obvious after only a couple of minutes drive. An ominous black cloud roiled in the otherwise blue sky. That it was centred over an unremarkable row of terraced houses did little to lessen the chilling effect. As they drew to a halt on the opposite side of the road, Alan reached out to close the cab's windows.

'No,' Mavis said, putting the yarn and nail back into her large carpet bag. 'Let it in, Alan. Best I know as much about it as possible.'

The cloud's shade enveloped them, a gloomy darkness fell and the street lamps fizzled briefly on and then, just as quickly, faded back into the black, the amber light sucked dry by smoky tendrils.

But Mavis wasn't looking up, or even down at the blue front door of No. 16 as it squatted deep in the shadow of the glowering cloud. She was facing the other way, eyeing that rarest of mythical beasts: a working BT phone box.

She handed a Thermos flask to Alan and rooted in her bag for a couple of extra travel cups. 'Three teas, please, Alan. One for you, you know how I like mine, and the third with one – no, better make it *two* sugars.'

She cracked open the cab door and shivered.

'You sure this is your department, Mavis?' Alan asked, his Mockney accent slipping somewhat and showing a hint of his long-buried Armenian upbringing.

'No, I don't suppose it is. But we're here now. Best make do.'

She edged her way carefully over to the phone booth. An advert for a Meat Inferno pizza hid the interior but beneath the door there was a glimpse of black-laced underskirt over a pair of scuffed DMs.

Mavis pulled the kiosk door open. 'Are you alright, dear?' she asked, as a pair of startled eyes peered up through charcoal eye-shadow streaked by tears.

'Ah...'

'Jessica, isn't it? I guess it was you who phoned... this... in?'

The girl, her black hair shot through with purple, silver pentagram earrings swinging in their circular hoops, nodded and slowly relaxed the knuckle-whitening grip she had around her knees.

'Come and have a nice cup of tea and tell me all about it.'

The telling didn't take long. She huddled on the kerb, the 'safe' side of the taxi, as Mavis perched on a garden wall overlooking No. 16 and Alan stood on the cab's runner, peering over the top.

'It was an accident,' Jessica mumbled, head bowed.

'You mean,' Mavis said, not unkindly, 'that you didn't expect it to work?'

The girl looked up through her fringe, her shoulders momentarily bunched.

'Well, at least your primary ward took.'

'Primary ward?'

'The thing that's holding it where it is, love,' Alan helpfully chipped in.

'I fear it won't hold for much longer,' Mavis said, as the double-glazed PVC windows pulsed. The front-door letter flap popped open and something long and purple snaked through, tasting the air.

Mavis pulled a yellowed candle stub from her cavernous bag. She had a half-dozen Ikea tea lights that would have done just as well, but then, she did have an audience.

'Jessica, my dear, I'm going to need something from you.'

Jessica nodded defeatedly and offered up her arm, a fresh white bandage scrappily tied and edged with red.

Mavis shook her head. 'No, not that; your tea cup, please. I need to see which way it will break.'

After peering intently at the pattern of leaves at the bottom of the tin cup, Mavis consulted her iPad. Ever since the British Library had digitised their occult section, she had been saved lugging around a trunk full of hefty books, but such easy access was a mixed blessing. Although much of the scanned content was palpable nonsense, there was, scattered amongst the alchemical instructions and obtuse lore, the occasional page of true power. And so, somewhere in the heart of No.16, sat Jessica's smartphone, the screen locked on a scanned image from a dusty French grimoire – a summoning spell.

She lit the candle, sprinkled a few herbs around the base, and chanted under her breath.

For a moment, the fabric of the stone-clad terrace seemed to disintegrate, each brick, each slate, floating free of its neighbour and, through the gaps, the three of them caught a glimpse of something rising up on squat, powerful legs. Through the roof, a pair of torn reptilian wings flexed, blood red, and eight – or quite possibly a lot more – tentacles writhed in front of a hidden head, rippling hungrily towards them. It was slipping its bonds, shaking itself free both of the physical restraints: the bricks, the mortar, the cavity wall insulation, and also of the magical ward that Jessica had invoked in its summoning.

Mavis reached out and with her bare fingers *snuffed* the candle.

There was a noise not unlike that of an elephant, minus the bones, dropped from a great height directly onto the hard concrete floor of Tate Modern's Turbine Hall.

Mavis ducked behind the body of the cab as a couple of tons of calamari and dragon blood splattered across the road and the stench of the grave passed over them.

The chill, dank air lifted and sunlight flooded blindingly back, as though a total eclipse had finished way before it was due. In the near distance, a bird nervously started up its song, only to peter out into embarrassed silence when it realised it was singing solo.

'May I borrow your phone, Alan?' Mavis asked.

Alan stood rooted to the spot, something purple dripping from his cheek, until she asked again and silently he handed it over.

She tapped quickly away and immediately a voice asked, 'Emergency: which service?'

'Eldritch Cleanup, please,' Mavis said.

'Eldritch... what?'

'It's on the list, dear. Authorisation code: Howard Phillips. Better get me an Environmental Disaster Squad as well,' she said, eyeing the splattered tentacles and ectoplasmic goo. 'And a Media Blackout Squad, *stat*.'

'What happens now?' Jessica asked, her voice small.

Mavis looked up at the gaping hole in the roof as a section of chimney plummeted into the smoking remains. 'Normally we go down the gas leak route. Any strange sightings are attributed to oxygen deprivation.'

'No, I mean... to me?'

Mavis peered over the top of her glasses. Jessica stood, pale, morose, and currently rather sticky, although the taxi and Alan had borne the brunt. And yet, this curiously-attired slip of a girl had summoned a real stinker of a Class 2 minor deity, with little more than a blood offering and a high resolution smartphone. She'd be dead if her ward hadn't held, but the point was, it had, for just long enough, anyway.

'Ever thought of being an apprentice?' she asked.

'Like on the telly?' Jessica said, '*You're fired?* an' all that?'

Mavis smiled. 'Yes, dear. Something like that.'

After the End of the World, Mother Bakes Cakes

When reality collapsed it took most everything with it: the High School, the shopping mall, the Interstate. One thing it didn't take away was my mother's need to entertain; if anything, that got even stronger. The old foreclosed house, which had once stood forlorn at the top of our street, shuffled up to be next door and, as it filled with all manner of mythical creatures, Mother would take round freshly baked cookies and invite them to drop by anytime for coffee.

I don't think Dad would have stood for it; some of them weren't exactly house-trained. But he was stranded in a Bates-style motel room somewhere on the outskirts of San Diego with only a phone line to connect him to our much larger pocket of reality, so there wasn't all that much he could do about it.

Though he couldn't hide his dismay when Mother decided, roughly two months after the collapse, that it must be Christmas Eve or thereabouts and, as traditions had to be upheld, there was nothing for it but to ask Satan to play Santa.

'Honey! Think what you're suggesting!' he pleaded.

'I have, dear. I have no desire to live through October twenty-fifth forever and, even if the calendar rewrites itself every morning, I've been counting and I make it Christmas Eve. Ish.'

'I don't have a problem with that. But do we really need a Santa?'

'Well, *yes*. I know the kids are almost grown up, but we've done it since... oh gosh, forever. We mustn't let mere circumstance change that.'

'Dammit, isn't there someone else who can play him?'

'Language, Bobby! You're on speaker-phone. And no, dear, I don't think there is. Malcolm is simply too young. As for the neighbours, they're all such odd shapes, except for Satan, of course. You know, hon, he's almost as tall and slim as you were when we first bought that Santa outfit. I think he's going to look quite dashing.'

'But he's Satan!'

'I'm sorry? What's the problem? You think he'll be too embarrassed, perhaps? He's a gentleman and a very polite gentleman at that, so I'm sure if the request had made him feel uncomfortable, he would have said so.'

'You've *already* asked him?'

'Well, yes. I was chatting over afternoon tea when I realised what the date is, or should be. I told him of our little traditions and he seemed enchanted by it all. Bobby dearest, please don't worry, he's charming, really. The kids love him. Besides, he's the only neighbour I can invite over for Christmas dinner, all the others have such peculiar diets.'

'But—'

'And of course we'll lay a place for you and put you on speaker-phone, so you can join in,' she added, diplomatically.

'Humph. A fat lot of fun that will be. A Pringles and Snickers festive dinner. Deep joy.' There was an abrupt click as he hung up. Like the wall calendar and our food stores which, overnight, reset to the exact state they'd been in at the point of collapse, Dad's motel mini-bar did the same. My idea of heaven, that, though Mother said he'd have to watch his waistline, what with all the empty calories and saturated fat. It didn't help that Dad set himself the daily challenge of drinking the mini-bar dry before it magically restocked itself.

Mother shooed us out from under her feet as she set to work preparing the Christmas dinner for the following day. I took the opportunity to visit the fairy who'd taken up residence in the shed. She wasn't in a good mood though, even when I begged her to tell me about the other pockets she'd visited.

The fairy said all the remaining pockets of reality were

different sizes and some pockets were even smaller than she was, which meant she wasn't sure what those ones contained.

She also said that none of the pockets were connected and it wasn't easy travelling between them. I pointed out that we talked to my dad every day, but she just sniffed and told me I didn't understand, that it had to do with conservation of information, which was far more important than energy or momentum. She said that because we were connected at the point when the collapse occurred, the connection couldn't simply vanish, but I didn't see why not, plenty had, like the rest of the houses in our street and half of the kids' playground, the end of the slide ending abruptly three feet above the ground, as I'd already found out to my cost.

The fairy said the collapse was fractal. She paused and gave me a hard stare. 'Fractal means—'

'I know what fractal means. Like a cauliflower.'

'That's just one example of fractal, this is different. Things vanished that, at the moment of collapse, weren't in the thoughts of the principals. And each of the principals... ah, it's too complicated for you, you're just a kid. Oh, for some real company.'

I wasn't offended, I knew she meant other fairies. As yet, none had turned up. The fairy says that any principals that could pass between the pockets as she could would eventually arrive here, in ours, because it was the largest by far. But I wondered if it wasn't my mother's cooking that lured them in and encouraged them to stay.

I suggested the fairy talked with Satan, but she scowled and told me once again, 'the horned one is not to be trusted'.

The first time she'd mentioned his horns I'd spent the next coffee morning studying Satan's hairline until my mother told me it was rude to stare. They were there all right, though not exactly obvious: tiny little nubs you'd easily mistake for stray tufts in his otherwise perfect hair.

When I got back the kitchen was quiet. I could hear something happening upstairs though, it sounded like someone was moving a piano. I went up cautiously; when you've unexpectedly come face to face with a harpy flapping around the bathroom early one morning you learn to be wary of such noises. But it was just Malcolm and Mother struggling to get the artificial tree down from the loft.

The rest of the evening was spent putting up the decorations, hoping they wouldn't reset themselves in the morning, and trying to work out what I could give Malcolm as a present.

Christmas Day broke, as ~~October 1q~~ twenty-fifth always did, bright and crisp and with a sheen of morning dew dusting the cobwebs on the lawn, the fall colours past their peak but the trees still clinging to their leaves. Or re-clinging to those that were destined to fall during the day and magically re-attach themselves sometime around midnight. Just after breakfast – pancakes and freshly baked croissants, also as usual – there was a sharp knock at the door and there stood Santa.

'Ho ho ho!' cried Satan, tugging at the fluffy white beard that covered his neat goatee. 'Merry Christmas! May I come in?'

I'd always thought it was vampires that couldn't enter uninvited, but Satan seemed to have the same issue. That or his asking was just another example of his impeccably old-fashioned manners.

Mother fussed over him, saying how wonderful it was that Santa had arrived so punctually, asking if he wanted a spiced tomato juice. Tomato was the only juice we happened to have in the fridge at the moment of the collapse. How I yearned for orange, for cranberry, or even for freshly pressed apple!

'The presents are under the tree ready to be handed out...' she said, and then stopped, wide-eyed. 'But Santa! What *do* you have in your sack?'

'Hmm? Ah yes, ho ho ho! I took the liberty of wrapping a few items, they're nothing really, mere trifles.'

'Oh, you shouldn't have. That's simply wonderful. But I

don't know if we have anything for you in return.' She cast her glance rapidly around the hallway and I saw her eyeing the brass barometer that hung on the wall. I guessed we wouldn't miss it, by now we all knew the readings by heart, though there would be hell to pay if Dad ever found out.

'Ho ho, that's really not necessary. As I understand it, sherry and mince pies are generally considered fair payment for Santa's deliveries?'

'Ah,' Mum looked downcast. 'There's no sherry I'm afraid and we don't have the ingredients for mince pies either.'

There was only so much she, supreme domestic goddess though she was, could do with what was currently available in her cupboards. The end had come, rather inconveniently, well before her usual shopping spree for dried fruits and nuts that announced the start of the festive baking season.

'Perhaps a slice of coffee cake instead?' she offered with a worried shrug.

With a flourish Satan whipped out a gift-wrapped box and matching bottle from his sack. 'Then – Ho ho ho! – I suggest you open these presents, first.'

I have to say, Satan played a very good Santa. He'd somehow managed to find Mother's favourite perfume: an apple shaped bottle of DKNY, and for Malcolm an old-style shaving kit, complete with one of those odd badger-hair brushes for the shaving cream. I teased my brother that a piece of Scotch tape was all he really needed to remove the wisps of fluff shadowing his lower face, but Santa boomed, 'No, no, no! Malcolm is growing up and before you know it he'll be a fine young gentleman. And you, Carol,' he said, turning to me, 'are already a beautiful young lady.'

With that he handed me a plain white box done up with a neat black bow. I can't say what I'd really expected, but I couldn't believe my eyes as I carefully folded back the tissue paper and found a little black dress covered in thousands of tiny black sequins. I rushed away to try it on; it was oh-so elegant, sequins shimmering as I twisted and turned in the full length mirror. It fitted perfectly and there was no way I was going to take the first new item of clothing I'd seen since the collapse off again, even if Mother did archly suggest it was perhaps *too* little of a little black dress.

But even Malcolm said I looked good in it and with Satan stood there beaming, she relented. I caught her glancing down and straightening the seams of her flour-dusted skirt, as if embarrassed by the comparison.

After he'd handed out the presents, Satan sat back in Dad's armchair with a glass of the sherry he'd provided and regaled us with tales of how his sleigh only had one reindeer, one runner, and no reins, and how difficult it was cornering under those circumstances. Pure nonsense, of course, but that was all part of the fun. Time flew and before I knew it Mother was dropping frantic hints in Satan's direction.

Finally he twigged. 'Well, Ma'am, Carol, Malcolm, be good, or goodish, at least. I must leave you now, many, um, more families to visit... Merry Christmas!'

With that and a wink, he left, only to return half an hour later dressed in a tux and sporting a dusty bottle of French wine.

'Châteauneuf-du-Pape, sixty-six,' he said, proudly. 'That's *sixteen*-sixty-six, of course, a time of fires and plagues and rampant superstition. Wonderful year. The vintage isn't bad, either.'

Mother apologised for the chicken Kievs, the closest thing to turkey her freezer contained, but Satan said it was all wonderful and how well they went with all the roasted vegetables. Dad joined in as best he could from afar, though his main contribution seemed to be the clink of miniatures and the slow steady crunch of salt and vinegar crisps. By the time we started on the autumn berry trifle, he'd finished everything he could eat or drink from the mini-bar and had decided to go and lie down for a bit.

Once we'd done justice to dessert, Satan chimed a long fingernail against a wine glass miraculously re-filled with its dark red liquid and made a little speech about how grateful he was to Mother for the splendid hospitality.

'And now, I believe it is traditional for us to retire to the living room while the kids clear the table, yes? Or perhaps, since it is such a warm um, *Christmas* day, the sunroom?'

A confused look flitted across Mother's face. 'Did I mention that as well? But–'

But Malcolm was already up and starting to pile plates on top of each other. 'Come on, sis.'

I watched Satan lead Mother out and wondered what they were playing at. I knew, even if Malcolm didn't, that this particular tradition was when Dad thanked Mother with some serious postprandial smooching. Surely that wasn't what Satan intended?

'Ah, Malcolm. I'll just go upstairs to change. I can't do dishes in a cocktail dress.' I said, and got quickly out of earshot before he could argue.

I went up, but I didn't go to my room, I crept into Dad's office instead. The window was already ajar and I knew that I'd be able to hear what was happening in the sunroom below. As I settled onto the window seat, I could hear Satan's deep baritone.

'–and the chicken Kievs, so much more interesting than turkey! What you manage with such limited resources is a source of constant amazement to me. Oh, here, let me rearrange that blanket. It's getting a bit cooler, don't you think?'

'As it does every evening at this time, regular as clockwork,' Mother sighed. 'Do you really think Carol and Malcolm are getting older? I wasn't sure that was possible.'

'They certainly are, Suzy.'

Suzy! I almost fell out the window. What had happened to *Ma'am*? To Satan's legendary politeness? How were they suddenly on first name terms?

'Although the day itself never changes,' he continued, 'the arrow of time marches on for all of the principals. If it didn't, you wouldn't remember what happened yesterday.'

Mother sniffed. 'Perhaps that would be better.'

'Oh no, dear sweet lady, don't say that. Your continuing and developing companionship is one of the few delights left to me. There, there, you're shivering. Here, let me put my arm around your shoulders.'

'Well, thank you. But if they are getting older...'

'Mmm. Yes, Suzy?'

'Oh! My, that feels good. A little lower if you please. Well then, what happens when they... y'know, hit puberty?'

'I'd say Carol is for all intents and purposes already there. And Malcolm isn't too far behind. Another year, perhaps. As for what happens, nature happens I suppose.'

'Nature? What do you mean, nature?' Mother's voice had risen an octave.

'Since I am an angel – fallen of course – and you, despite being the very embodiment of an Earth goddess, are a post-menopausal woman whose husband and head of the family is stranded half a world away, your children are the only humans capable of breeding left in existence. Ha ha, kind of like Adam and Eve in the garden of Eden, wouldn't you say?'

There was a noise, the sound of a wicker chair being sharply pushed back across the flagstone floor. I guessed my mother was now standing. 'But that can't be!'

'It can't? Why not?' Another scrape of a chair and now Satan was standing as well: I could just see the crown of his head, the little horns surprisingly visible from above.

'That's incest! They're brother and sister, I won't allow it.'

'Then you must forbid it. Oh, Suzy, Ma'am, please sit back down. I didn't mean to upset you, please forgive me. And on second thoughts, perhaps it might be best if you didn't mention it at all? I mean, forbidding it *might* put the idea in their heads, which is the last thing– is that someone shouting?'

Satan turned and stared in my direction. I ducked down,

hoping he hadn't seen me. He couldn't have known I was there, could he? Crouched below the window seat I heard Malcolm calling for me, fed up of doing the dishes on his own.

I changed out of the dress as fast as I could, my thoughts a whirlwind, not even bothering to hang the stupid, slinky thing up, angry with Satan, annoyed that the presents he had brought each of us had been merely part of his scheming. A shaving kit for Malcolm? A sophisticated black dress for me? Adult presents for kids!

But I supposed, if we were getting older as Satan had said and if this was indeed Christmas, then at some point we'd missed Malcolm's fifteenth birthday. When *did* boys grow up? He certainly hadn't started acting like a mature, responsible adult, but then, Mother said most boys *never* did, usually with a pointed glance at Dad.

Back in the kitchen I grabbed a tea towel and started drying, staring at the pimply back of my brother's neck. Me and Malcolm as Adam and Eve: what was Satan smoking? I would never have even entertained the idea. If I was going to have a crush on anyone, it would be *him*, all lean-bodied, widow's-peaked, red-skinned, gift-bearing and immaculately dressed (even in a daft suit-and-beard-combo) six foot two, smooth talking devil of him, and certainly not my soppy and frankly dull-as-dishwater younger sibling.

At least, that was, or *would* have been, the case before today; before Satan started putting the moves on Mother. It was a good thing he'd so blatantly blown it, with his disgusting talk about breeding. Ugh.

Men! I fumed, banging the baking tray back into the oven so hard that Malcolm turned and stared at me. I scowled and stuck out my tongue.

The fairy had been right all along: he wasn't to be trusted. And the fact Dad wasn't going to be back anytime soon, if ever, just showed Santa – oops! I mean *Satan* – for the cunning evil little snake in the grass he damn well was!

Time, The Devourer

If you ask me, Midas had it easy.

My name is Helene and I am the daughter of a God. Or so my mother always told me. Her husband, a Captain in Delian League, was not impressed by the divine miracle he returned home to and so, at the unusually early age of seven, I became an acolyte at the Temple of Aphrodite.

The High Priestess recruited only the most beautiful acolytes and, as I grew, it became obvious that I was the most beautiful of them all. But serving from such an age it was also clear that beauty does not last. I saw many a weeping woman cast out of the Temple as the first blemishes of middle age appeared.

I vowed this would not happen to me. I devoted myself to studying every means of halting time's cruel effects. The charlatans who sold me their expensive charms and potions pandered to my obsession and I reached the point where I was convinced I would live forever. I gloated that my beauty would never fade and would always be on par with Aphrodite's.

In the middle of her Temple, right in front of her altar.

So yes, of course the jealous bitch heard me.

Her punishment was a curse: a most peculiar, vindictive curse. In some ways you could say I was granted my heart's desire; I would never grow old, my beauty would never fade. But at what a cost!

Flowers withered in my hand. Wine soured and bread went mouldy. Plaster crumbled from the walls of the Temple and my wooden bed collapsed rotten beneath me. Worse than all of this, when my friend Phoebe tried to comfort me, her skin dulled and creased, liver spots appearing before my eyes. Her legs creaked as she tried to stand, not certain what had just happened, her youth and beauty a ruin.

Everything I touched faded, aged, perished. Tempus edax rerum: Time, the devourer of all things. Even my clothes fell to tatters and, naked, I too was banished from the Temple. Everywhere I sought refuge death and decay swiftly followed. I would walk through a field and the wheat would shrivel on the stalk, pass a farm and the milk would curdle. I retreated to the hills, where I could do less damage.

And there, in a golden cave, I found Midas.

He was not happy to see me. 'Go away,' he whined. 'Or else you'll be turned to gold.'

'Go away yourself,' I retorted. 'Or else you'll be turned to old.'

We stared at each other for a moment, before both of us reached the same inevitable conclusion and we embraced, eager for mutual oblivion.

It did not come. Not only were we immune to our own curses, we were also unaffected by each other's. The Gods would not release us from our punishment so easily. I disengaged his hands from where they had wandered and he shrugged and retired to his golden bed.

I've tried, but I really can't imagine a wetter dishcloth to spend the rest of eternity with. Kings his age ought to be hitting their stride, but he shuffled about with a forlorn gait, showing all the uncertainty and poor judgement that he was rightfully famous for.

But, there isn't all that much you can do when anything that isn't gold disintegrates in your hands and your only companion's idea of conversation is to ask whether he was richer than Croesus yet. After an uncounted number of centuries, I had a moment of weakness and gave in.

Disgust turned to horror as I realised I was pregnant.

Midas didn't seem particularly concerned.

'How will I care for it?' I wailed. 'What if the child is born and I touch it, and it ages and dies? Or what if you touch it and it turns to gold?'

'Then you won't have to care for it anymore,' he replied. 'Look on the bright side, there are worse fates. What if you have a child that never grows up? What if you remain pregnant forever?'

I'd have hit him, the miserable sod, if he hadn't effectively been wearing gold body armour.

As my belly swelled, the hunger pains that I could never satisfy doubled in intensity. I didn't see how a child could grow inside me, when everything I tried to eat turned to dust in my mouth, but it did. I wondered if I'd be able to nurse it, when the time came, or would it starve at my breast? All the while, Midas clumped about in his heavy slippers, exhaling motes of gold that sparkled in the sunlight, and telling me that I looked fat.

Given half a chance he would have slunk off when the contractions began, but I sure as hell wasn't letting him. Not that he was much help, not that either of us really knew what we were doing. I had not thought it possible for anything to hurt so much! But finally, Midas stood, cradling something in his hands, a terrible expression on his face. And then he turned and showed the little golden baby to me and I screamed in anguish.

The baby screamed back. It was the Gods' last laugh. From then onwards, Jason's glow faded; his skin turned pink and even his fleecy golden hair turned black. And we found that we were no longer cursed.

Midas had been preparing himself for this day. He'd been hoarding rocks he'd turned to gold in great piles at the back of the cave. He was going to build – or buy – himself a new Kingdom, but get it right this time. He waxed lyrical on how many rooms his palace would have, how many wives, and how big his kitchens would be, and how many wives.

I had to gently point out that the apples and other fruit we were eating had once been gold, as had the clothes I was now wearing. His face went ashen and he rushed to the back of the cave. I stood safely to one side as rocks came flying past and then he re-emerged, wild-eyed, with a scant armful of still golden nuggets.

'No time to waste!' he cried and went haring down the hill towards the nearest town.

I found him at the bottom of a ravine, his neck at an unnatural angle, dull rocks scattered about him. I buried him there, a cairn from his previously precious stones marking the grave.

When the food finally ran out, I salvaged the few items that were, it turned out, genuinely gold, and carefully descended to the plains below, with Jason in a makeshift sling.

Oh how strange it was. What changes time had wrought! Even the language was different; a few odd words were all that I could recognise. I could not make myself understood and, after hours of wandering aimlessly around the town, I found myself sobbing on the steps of a temple, where a priest, seeing the crying babe in my arms, took pity and gave me shelter.

I had thought once, that my curse was eternal. I had no way then of knowing that even the Gods are not forever. The priest taught me his language and tried to teach me his religion as well. But the strange, crucified figure left me cold and he in return refused to listen to my tales of Zeus, of Apollo, and of Aphrodite.

With the last of the golden jewellery, I opened up a beauty salon. And though I can't really afford to do so, I find myself turning away the pretty young girls of the town, berating them for their empty-headed vanity. Fortunately, there are plenty of older housewives eager – desperate – to be pampered. Most of my payment is in food, or in clothes, but that's okay. I've seen enough gold to last a lifetime.

Jason has grown and keeps growing. He's turning into a fine young man. It's only what you would expect; after all; he is the son of a King and a Divine Priestess, and was born on a golden bed.

I don't tell him that.

I tell him his father died in the haunted hills and his eyes widen and he asks what haunts them? I tell him nothing, not any more.

And that's it really. I guess it's a very ordinary end to an extraordinary tale. One last thing, though. The other day Jason found me at my mirror, smiling like an idiot. He asked me why and I showed him the grey hair I had just found.

He didn't understand; but it was the most wonderful thing in the world.

Bring Rope

> *bring rope*

I texted back a single question mark, but there was no reply.

*

Julia lived in a converted warehouse out Docklands way. The artists weren't supposed to live in their studios, but, London rents being London rents and artists being artists, most of them had a chaise longue, a pull-out sofa, or some other suitably bohemian arrangement. Julia and I, we had an on-off thing, so much so that I wondered if I should have put a winky grin after the question mark, but most likely one of her fellow artists needed a chunky piece of salvage lifted, or some completed 'artwork' lowered.

Chances were I'd not see the rope again and I weighed this against any possible return of favour from Julia. Then I remembered I had a climbing rope I didn't exactly trust anymore, so I chucked that in my rucksack.

I was expecting Julia to buzz me in at the gate, but instead the crackly intercom voice told me: 'I'll come down.'

I twiddled my thumbs for a couple of minutes, listening to the distorted sound of someone's radio cranked up to maximum volume, before she appeared and let me through. 'Jeez Jules!' I said. 'You been working lates?'

She looked haggard, her hair a mess and her face thinner than I remembered, eyes darker. She took one step forward and buried herself in a hug before breaking off and pointing at my bag.

'Got the rope?' she asked. I nodded and she chewed her lip. 'Come up,' she said. 'Got something to show you.'

All of which under other circumstances might have been highly promising, but we turned off before we reached her floor and entered darkened corridors I'd not been down before. The old tobacco warehouse had been carved up into odd-shaped rooms, plywood passageways hacked between them any which way. But these corridors were more permanent and less lived in: no artwork adorned the walls, no lights shone behind the scant few doors, old newspapers and last autumn's leaves disintegrated quietly in the corners.

Julia yanked on a metal door, the hinges screamed in protest, and everything I'd imagined I might be about to see, disappeared.

'What the...'

The words dried up and I just stood and stared.

We were in an unconverted part of the warehouse. Wide and tall, it went all the way to the corrugated roof, three floors up. In the middle of this vast open space hung a cloud: a black, featureless, utterly impossible cloud. Beneath it a gabble of the community's artist-types hung wearily onto ropes that arced upwards and vanished into the inky nothingness.

Julia threaded her way between them to where a length of coarse rope lay untidily on the concrete floor. She picked up one end and threw it towards the cloud. At first I thought she'd missed – it was a clumsy, lazy throw – but the cloud snapped up the offering and pulled the rope taut with Julia gripping the other end.

'Now you,' she said.

I stared at her. Stared at the mind-warping cloud, at the other artists. Stared and slowly shook my head.

'Thomas!' she called out, breaking the spell. I dropped my bag and hauled out the climbing rope, untying the simple knot at its heart and pulling a section free. Holding on to it with my left hand I threw the coiled loops as hard as I could with my right and watched as it was taken up just as eagerly as Julia's was. I tested the rope; the pull wasn't a strong one, enough to lift my arm if I let it, but not enough to make me strain.

I looked around once again at the others and then at Julia, whose eyes were now half closed. There were a dozen people in the room, artists who could and would chew the fat about anything, any time of the day, and who were only normally this silent and still when they were stoned out of their artsy little minds.

'Julia!' I hissed. She turned slowly towards me. 'What are we doing here?'

She blinked, looked up towards the hovering darkness, gestured with her chin. 'Holding it down,' she said.

I thought about that for a while. I'm not sure how long. Time had a weird way of slipping by when you looked into the heart of that cloud.

'Why don't we just tie off the ropes?' I suggested.

She gave me a small, wry grin. 'Try it.'

I eased over to the wall where there was a metal loop embedded in the brickwork. A quick figure of eight later I turned back to the watching Julia, letting go of the rope. As I did so it slackened and the end suspended in the cloud dropped back to Earth, bouncing off the shoulder of one of the artists who shuffled sleepily away from it.

'You need to keep hold of it,' Julia said. 'Skin on rope. Otherwise, it does that.'

I untied the knot and made ready to send the loose end back up into the cloud. 'What if I don't?' I said. 'What if you all... let go?'

She shrugged. 'Have you looked into it? Deep into it?'

I nodded.

'How does it make you feel?'

I looked again. Its centre was a total absence of light or form, but the peripheries... the peripheries held swirling shapes that eluded description, tendrils of inky blackness that vanished as soon as I turned my attention on them, that gave rise to strange, dark, magical thoughts. I couldn't tell you what these thoughts contained; they were as ethereal as the half-glimpsed forms.

They held an odd attraction though, like the gentle pull on my arms, the pull that kept the rope tight, the rope I couldn't even remember having thrown again.

I turned to try and explain these vague thoughts to Julia and was surprised to see more people had arrived: our numbers had doubled. Some were in painters' smocks, others in dressing gowns, one in just his boxers, all linked to the cloud by whatever ropes they had managed to scrounge up.

'Julia,' I said, and her head reluctantly lifted once again from its slumped position. 'Where did this... *thing*... come from?'

It must have been a full minute before she jerked her shoulders and broke her glazed eyes from mine. 'I think Stefan made it.'

I looked to where she'd gestured. Most of the artists were in a rough circle fanning out around the fringes of the cloud, around the edges of the room, but Stefan stood alone directly beneath it. Though 'stood' wasn't quite right: the toes of his shoes dragged across the concrete, his arms spread wide as he hung from the pair of ropes clenched in his outstretched hands. I blinked. It looked like he was being crucified.

Maybe it was that. Maybe it was the unnatural stillness of all those people not talking, or eating, or drinking, or even smoking. Maybe it was because I didn't see the same thing they did when I stared into the cloud, my eyes closed to the artistic inspiration it offered them.

Whatever it was, I wanted out: a sudden, desperate urge to be elsewhere.

I felt Julia's eyes watching me and I looked back at her, feeling small, feeling guilty. 'I'll, um, call a friend to come help, shall I?'

She nodded, just once. Didn't smile. Didn't say anything. But she knew. I forced my hand to let go and watched the snake of the rope fall between the artists. No-one stirred. I turned, leaving my bag, leaving the rope, aware of the dark void at my back. As I walked out I raised my mobile to my ear, though I hadn't called anyone, though there wasn't anyone I could possibly call.

Outside a surreal dawn was breaking, the clouds lit pink, the whirr of an electric milk van and a few forlorn birds the only signs of life. With a shaking hand I reached for a smoke, but my bag was upstairs, with Julia, with the blackness. I felt drained, exhausted. The pit of my stomach was a hollow I was too weary to think about filling, but I couldn't ignore my thirst, nor the urgent need for a toilet.

I thought of going back into the studios, up to Julia's room; I knew where she kept the spare key. I thought of going back into that cavernous space with its black, empty heart and dragging Julia out of there. Dragging everybody out of there.

But I did none of those things. I ducked behind a skip to relieve myself and then got the DLR to Bank, mingling with the early-morning commuters, doing my best to blink away the darkness lingering behind my eyelids, the darkness I could see wherever I looked.

*

I left a few messages for Julia. Tried to call her once or twice, but got no reply. I didn't try again. I guess I was wary of what she'd think of me for having bailed. It wasn't my fault. She must have realised that I didn't have an artistic bone in my body, must have known that I always listened carefully to what other people said before voicing any opinions on the splattered mess of their meaningless paintings, their tatty sculptures or, worst of all, the reclaimed junk that made up their 'installations'. She must have known that even my interest in her own dismal daubs was entirely feigned, and why.

It was almost a week before I summoned up the nerve to reclaim my climbing bag. The rope I didn't care about, but the rucksack was nearly new and it had a couple of carabiners and a belaying loop that I could ill afford to lose.

The courtyard was quiet, nobody around. Nobody around at all. I pressed the buzzer but there was no buzz, no answer, and when I pushed the gate it opened freely, the magnetic lock inactive, the power out. The stairwell was dark, the timer switch for the lights did nothing but slowly, mechanically, wind down. Which was kind of creepy though it wasn't so dark you couldn't see. Wasn't as dark as that cloud. Nothing was.

It took me a while to find my way back to that gaping space. I pushed the protesting door half open, my heart pounding, and squeezed through, dreading what I was about to see.

There was nothing. No cloud, no people, no climbing bag, and no ropes. No dust or cobwebs or leaves either. It looked like the place had been swept spotlessly clean. I crossed to the centre of the room, staring up to the skylit roof, peering at the walls, looking for any sign of anything at all.

Two floors up I let myself into Julia's workshop. It was cold and lifeless somehow, even though it was still full of her artwork, her clothes, her empty bottles of wine. I ran a finger over the hardened acrylic on a paintbrush, glanced into a coffee cup whose dregs had long since dried and cracked. Up the ladder in the attic space where she had her mattress I picked up a T-shirt of mine, left behind on a previous visit, or maybe she'd borrowed it after an impromptu stopover at my place. It felt damp and musty and I let it drop where I'd found it.

*

The story broke the day after: Mysterious Disappearances at Artist Studios, 12 missing. 12 pictures on the double page spread, none of whom were Julia.

I kept quiet. A few of the missing turned up in the weeks that followed, though none of them had been at the studios for a while. And a lot more names were added, Julia's included, but who knew what the real tally is?

*

As far as I know, I'm the only person who saw the cloud and hasn't vanished into whatever hell they all went to. There's no-one to talk to about it, no-one to ask if they see the same black abyss when they close their eyes at night, if they feel their soul slipping into its gaping maw as they try desperately to sleep, if they wake with the same numbing sense of loss, the same emptiness reflected back in the bathroom mirror.

Except for Stefan, perhaps.

I saw his photo in someone else's Evening Standard, assumed he was a latecomer to the roll call of the missing. But it wasn't his disappearance that got him into the papers, it is his triumphant emergence onto the premier stage of art. Stefan has been commissioned to fill the Turbine Hall at the Tate Modern.

The art world is in shock: the biggest, most exclusive space in London, given to a nobody. No track record, no Turner prize, no previous exhibitions of any note.

A fraud or a PR stunt is suspected, rumour rife that 'Stefan Wilkowitz' is Banksy's real name, or perhaps a pseudonym adopted for this singular work.

People gather to see the huge screens behind which he labours, even though the piece isn't due to open for another week. The dearth of information just adds to the hype, just adds to the building excitement.

Really, there's only one thing anyone knows about him, or his art. It's the name of his installation and his instruction to all who eagerly await its opening. It's on the personalised invitation to the exclusive preview that dropped, unexpectedly, through my letter box this morning. And it's emblazoned across the glass top of Tate Modern for all to see, in fourteen foot high, dark-as-the-night letters.

'Bring Rope', it says.

Temp

'Nice scythe,' the bumblebee said.

'Thanks,' mumbled John.

The problem with Halloween wasn't deciding what to wear, or even travelling to a party looking like an idiot, it was that once you arrived and everyone had seen your costume, you still had to stay in it for the rest of the evening.

The thin black cloak wasn't so bad – you could at least lower the hood – but the scythe must have been seven feet tall. John thought about stowing it in the bedroom along with the coats, but he feared it wouldn't be there when he returned, and, strictly speaking, it wasn't his to lose.

The girl in the bumblebee outfit ran a thumb over the keen blade. 'Ooh! It's sharp!'

That was another thing. When he'd found it propped up in the alley behind his apartment, it had been pitted with rust, but now it gleamed under the kitchen's halogen spotlights.

And then there was the odd dream he'd had of hours spent hunched over a spinning whetstone, showers of sparks illuminating the night and a grinding noise like the scream of a thousand lost souls piercing his skull as the edge took shape. What was all that about?

The bumblebee was cute. Slim, short hair, mischievous grin. Just his type, if she hadn't been so obviously out of his league. But she'd made two attempts to start a conversation, and *she* didn't know he wasn't some ultra-hip media tycoon, did she?

'So,' he tried hard to think of something original to say, and failed, 'what do you do?'

'Besides making honey?' she laughed, a pleasing lilt to her

114

voice. 'I run a temp agency.'

'Ah.'

'Ah?' she echoed, one black eyebrow raised.

'Ah…well, I suppose,' he floundered, 'difficult times for you?'

She shrugged. 'Not really. When there are redundancies, there are always temporary shortages of skills and resources. Usually just someone to help clear a backlog, or to hold the fort while an employee is sick or on vacation.'

'Like… substitute teachers?'

She frowned. 'Well, something along those lines, but I'm actually rather more specialised. I don't do teachers, or secretaries, or' – she looked him up and down – 'data entry clerks.'

His heart sank.

'I only deal with the top end of the market. Afraid I can't tell you who my clients are. Customer confidentiality and all that.' She shrugged again, then looked up at him expectantly. 'Do my wings do anything when I do that?'

'Do it again,' he suggested, a lump in his throat.

She did, an amused look on her face. 'Anything?'

He shook his head, his lips dry. 'No,' he said slowly. 'Not behind you, anyway.'

She threw a playful punch at his arm. 'Naughty! But I'm afraid I'll have to love you and leave you now, John. I'm actually working tonight and I have another two parties to visit.'

He stared into his drink. He shouldn't be disappointed – he should ask for her number. But he never had been good at that stuff. Besides, he didn't even know her name. He couldn't even remember telling her his. And how did she know he was a data entry clerk?

'Aw, don't worry,' she said cheerfully. 'I'm sure I'll see you again.' She tapped a black and yellow striped fingernail against the edge of the scythe. 'You do make an awfully good grim reaper.' And then she left.

He wandered aimlessly around the party. People seemed to

make way for him without actually acknowledging his existence. He didn't mind; he hardly knew anyone there. He'd once worked with the host's ex-girlfriend, who'd been a bit liberal with her Facebook invites.

Even with the strict fancy dress code, the place was heaving. As John made his way to the small roof terrace, a Smurf and a zombie were erecting a barricade of bookcases at the front door to prevent any late arrivals.

Outside, despite the cold weather, things were only marginally better. The partygoers would probably have spilled over onto the wrought iron fire escape if it hadn't been chock-full of building materials – plaster board, wooden planks, bottles of varnish and turpentine.

He passed a couple of Guy Fawkes, complete with V for Vendetta masks, who were drunkenly trying to set up a firework the size of a microwave. It was, he was sure, likely to end in disaster.

A sudden image came to him: a fiery inferno, flames curling around the top of the walls to meet at the ceiling, a curtain of white heat. People fighting to escape, screaming, burning. Through it all, a dark figure striding, untouched by the flames, bending over fallen figures, a blade glowing red above his head. An angel of mercy. The scythe did not maim or kill; it performed a compassionate service, severing the thin ribbon of light that kept tortured souls anchored to blackened bodies.

He blinked, stunned by his vision, as Guy Fawkes One handed Guy Fawkes Two a yellow plastic lighter.

In the pale moonlight his hands appeared washed of colour, thin and cold, and he thrust them deep into the pockets of the heavy black cloak. He couldn't remember putting anything into those pockets – couldn't remember there being pockets – but from the left he withdrew a thin card that seemed to glow in the wan light.

Sarah Bartholomew, it read, the *B* a stylised bumblebee,

glittering like a wintry cobweb. *Recruitment and Resource Management.*

From the right, his bleached skeletal arm pulled an antique hourglass. Even as he watched, the last grains of sand fell through the narrow neck. As they did, a church bell rang out a mournful midnight and the sky was lit up by a shower of falling sparks. The last chime was drowned out by the soft whoomph of ignition.

John nodded solemnly. Time to go to work.

Mechanical

'Knight to B4,' von Kempelen said, his English only lightly accented.

The itch on the end of my nose was getting worse but I ignored it, just as I ignored the urge to lift the edge of the blindfold. My hand still smarted from the last attempt and if I hadn't been promised payment I'd have jacked it in, then and there. My stomach rumbled. This stupid game had gone on far too long.

'Bishop to E5 – revealed check,' I replied. I heard the wooden piece clacking down to its new home on the board and a half grunt from my opponent.

'King to–'

'C7?' I interrupted. 'Unwise. Knight to D5: checkmate. Your best move is pawn to B3, but it will cost you your queen. You should have taken the exchange when you had the chance.'

'My, you are the impatient one. Still, you may remove the blindfold, Miss...?'

How little they thought of me to forget my name already. 'Haley,' I said as I pulled away the strip of dark cloth. 'Sarah Haley, and I believe you owe me a half-crown, Herr von Kempelen!'

I had not expected the lazy smile with which this was met and my fingers almost flew to the blade I kept hidden in the lining of my coat.

'All in good time,' von Kempelen drawled. 'Tell me, Miss Haley, what is your height?'

'My height?' I coughed. 'What the devil?'

'Five foot two, wouldn't you say, Mister Doyle?'

Mr Doyle spoke for the first time since he'd blindfolded me. 'Five-one, Sir, and either ninety-three or ninety-four pounds. I'll stake a shilling on it.'

'Well, you're the expert, Mr Doyle,' von Kempelen said. 'Mr Doyle was a hangman and a very good one, before he found his way to me. You know how a hangman judges the weight of the condemned?'

I shuddered as I remembered Mr Doyle's firm handshake. 'Now look–'

'Calm yourself, Miss Haley. Mr Doyle, a half-crown if you will. But if you want more – a half-crown a day plus food and lodgings – then come see me tomorrow, at five o'clock.'

I caught the coin as it flew across the smoky room but I didn't move, not yet. A girl has to put up with a lot to make it in this world and I preferred the games to remain firmly on the chequered board.

'Is this about the Turk?' I asked, defiantly.

'Ah!' von Kempelen grinned. 'It seems our reputation precedes us, Mr Doyle.'

Of course it did. The Mechanical Turk was the sensation of the day. I'd learnt about it from my father, God rest his soul, but back then it was reported irreparably broken, until it had reappeared over the Channel in Paris a little under a year ago. And now here it was, newly arrived in London.

'If you're going to ask me to play against the Turk, Sir,' I said, 'I don't need to come back tomorrow to decide. I'll gladly do it.'

'Good girl!' von Kempelen smiled. 'You'll take my pay then and come into my service. But there are two things you need to know. The first, is that my business is my business. I will not stand for loose talk and the disclosure of the secrets of any of my inventions will not go unpunished. You can, I trust, keep a secret?'

'I can. If the pay is regular?'

'It is.' He held out his hand and I looked at it suspiciously.

He had yet to tell me the other "thing" I needed to know. Still, a half-crown a day was a persuasive argument and I assumed we would go no further unless I agreed. I shook.

'And the second thing?' I asked, our hands still joined.

His smile stretched from ear to ear. 'Why, Miss Haley, I don't want you to play the Turk. I want you to *be* the Turk!'

*

I suppose it should have been obvious. The Turk, the chess-playing automaton, the mechanical wonder of the century, was a fraud. A very clever one, but a fraud nonetheless. The clockwork mechanisms did little but mask the fact that there was still space enough for an operator contained within. It took me a while to master the controls: the magnetic counters on the underside of the chess board, the shielded lamp so that I might see the levers, the pulleys for the Turk's arm and head. I had to learn to move swiftly and silently from compartment to compartment, while the innards of the Turk were revealed to the audience before each game, the wooden panels opened in turn to show light all the way through.

I learnt from Pierre, a homesick Frenchman whose trembling frame and pale white face belied a fierce intelligence, the only man I could never beat on the chessboard. But he was a broken man. I heard him whimpering in his sleep at night and the way his hollowed eyes kept darting to the doors and windows as if looking for an escape, for a desperate return to the wife and kids he oft talked about, had me doubling my efforts to master the Turk's operation.

While I learnt, I was paid nothing but board and lodging, the half-crown withheld until I was fit for the job for which I had been employed. My door was kept locked at night, excused with a silent smile by the ever-present, hulking Doyle. Still, I wouldn't have missed it for the world. I attended every performance, watching the way the crowd gasped and shrank back the first time the metal arm moved, the way they laughed when the Turk shook his head as he corrected an illegal move. I learnt von Kempelen's polished spiel, the explanation for the Turk's robes and turban, the 'traditional costume of an oriental sorcerer', he proclaimed, all the while masking the true origin of the smoke from the lamp by which Pierre operated.

At last, I played von Kempelen once more, this time as the Turk and, evidently having performed to his satisfaction, was told that the very next day I would finally take Pierre's place.

I expected Pierre to be happy – surely this would mean he'd be able to go home – but he just gave me a half-smile and retired early for the night, rubbing his bony back and not even playing our customary evening game.

I won't go into detail of that nerve-wracking first session, the way the smoke sometimes escaped into the compartment making my eyes water, the cramps, the slow build-up of heat, or the fact that for the last hour I played with something sharp sticking into my side. Despite it all, I emerged into a grey dusk, giddy with excitement at having played and beaten so many men, men who would otherwise never have deigned to play against a mere girl of seventeen years. I was sure I'd played the best chess of my life. I'd played aggressively and won, freed from the obligation to not show up my male opposition, freed from the fear of retribution. A heady feeling that evaporated when I saw the patch of blood soaking the dark shapeless shirt I wore. Doyle's eyes lit up when he saw the injury, but von Kempelen was quick to reassure me.

'We'll have that fixed immediately – it must be a loose strut. The Turk needs constant maintenance, constant repairs. Where were you when...?'

I pointed vaguely into the Turk's dark interior, though in the area I indicated there was no metal work to be seen. 'Perhaps Pierre–'

'Pierre is no longer with us,' Von Kempelen said.

I looked at him, surprised. 'He's not?'

'He boarded a packet boat for Calais after watching your first game. It seems he was more than happy with your operation, my dear.'

I flitted my eyes between the pair of them, but Doyle's were back to their impassive norm and von Kempelen's piercing gaze held no clues as to why he was lying. You don't live by the Thames all your life without learning something about the tides.

'You will be fit to play again tomorrow, I trust?' von Kempelen said, with a note of the imperative.

I nodded. 'Of course.'

*

My sleep was destroyed by black dreams, dreams of armies of mechanical men. Men clothed in turbans and cloaks, wielding sharp blades, curved like the crescent of the moon, plunging them over and over into my side. Sometime during the long night I thought I heard voices, thought I saw a light briefly appear and disappear, felt a draught stir the stale air around my cot.

'You said you'd fixed it!' one voice said.

'I did,' a tired voice replied. 'These are not... the same.'

'How can that be?'

'I don't know. I just don't know. I thought after Pierre...'

'We can't go on like this!'

'Can we not? Operators are cheap and with each, the Turk gets stronger. Besides, this is as much out of my hands as yours. Blame the Emperor, if you must, but never forget that somewhere out there, there is an executioner ready to measure both of us up for what happened in Vienna.'

*

That was the last time I saw the Turk, or von Kempelen, or mercifully, Mr Doyle. They should have realised that someone who could fit into the Turk's small compartments, might find an alternative way out of their lodgings, other than via the secured door.

I slipped out an hour before dawn, my knife making short work of the catch on the tiny window. Trembling in the cold, my coat and other winter clothes left behind, I traded my necklace for a place on the first coach to Oxford and from there walked the eight weary miles to Abingdon, where my uncle, a printer, lived. It was hard to leave London, harder still to become little more than a menial drudge at my Uncle's beck and call, keeping as low a profile as I could manage.

'Didn't you used to play chess?' he asked, one day. 'My brother–'

I shook my head vehemently. 'No sir, I was never any good at it.'

'A pity,' he said. 'It would have at least shown a spark of intelligence. Might have got you married and out of my hands. Though who'd take a frail, dull thing like you, I don't know.'

*

I stayed until I heard the news that the Turk had left England, destined for Leipzig. My uncle laughed when I asked where Leipzig was, his laugh fading to a puzzled stare when he saw the broadsheet in my hand. The dolt still assumed I couldn't read, though I'd been fixing up his mistakes since the day I'd arrived.

I left him the next morning, heading back to London, to the printing houses there, a forged letter of recommendation and my ink-stained fingers as references. I changed my name and played the wide-eyed country girl in the capital for the first time.

For a while, I followed the news about the Turk as it toured the European cities, wondering when it would be exposed. It never was, not even after it returned to Vienna and the news fell silent. Even so, I never dared reveal the Turk's secret, or return to the chessboard that I loved so much, never forgetting the feel of Mr Doyle's meaty hand around mine.

I suppose von Kempelen still owes me a half-crown, now I come to think about it, for my one day as the Turk. But I'll waive that gladly, in return for my life, and my immortal soul.

Gean Cánach

Not all monsters wear their evil on the outside.

Not all of them have sharp teeth and wicked claws and scaly hides.

Some have thick black hair on their handsome heads and wear fine tailored suits. Some have a kiss you would die for.

Literally.

I didn't believe it at first. How could my love, my Angela, be stolen from me by a man? Stolen so completely that she couldn't live without him?

I held her hand as she faded away, the doctors baffled by what could only be described as a broken heart.

And, on the day she died, I vowed revenge on this beast, this Gean Cánach of Celtic legend.

I prepared carefully.

Taking the longest knife from the kitchen, I cut out my heart. It hurt; it hurt like hell, but I was already in pain.

I changed my usual attire. Gone were the Doc Martens, fully half of my piercings, and the battered leather jacket. In their place, I donned one of Angela's flowery summer dresses. When I looked in the mirror, despite my short hair, I was a different woman.

And then I went searching. In this interconnected age, with Google and Facebook and Twitter, it wasn't hard.

When I laid eyes upon him, my heart – one hundred and seventy miles away and tucked safely in the freezer – leapt. He was all that Angela had described: dark and handsome, but so much more. Lips curved into a mocking, teasing smile. Eyes green and glittering. If his ears were a little long, they were well hidden by waves of his jet-black hair.

He knew he was beautiful, knew the effect he had on women. Knew that I would go to him when he oh-so-casually beckoned.

I hated him with every ounce of my body.

And yet, when we stood cheek to cheek, him the taller but only by an inch, when I breathed in his heady musk, even I was almost lost. But then I remembered the withered form of my true love.

As he swooned in to plant his poisonous kiss, the one that would seal my fate, that would have me pine to nothing when he assuredly left, I met it with the same cold steel with which I had carved out my heart.

So now my freezer contains his head: emerald eyes that still glitter, though for other reasons. His head, and my heart.

But it wasn't enough. Evil though he may have been, was he any worse than other men? Those who pretend love to innocent girls, who toy with their emotions, knowing all is false?

My task had only just begun.

Not all monsters wear their evil on the outside.

Not all of them have sharp teeth and claws and scaly hides.

Some have short hair and wear flowery dresses.

And some carry eight-inch carving knives in their wicked hands.

The Painted Platform

There once was a rich and powerful man who was desirous of a wife. He was so rich and so powerful that he could chose any wife he wanted – plain or beautiful, commoner or noble; none would dare say no to him.

But this was not enough for the rich and powerful man. He wanted to marry someone who could look past his chests of gold and his caskets of precious stones, who wasn't influenced by the vast lands he owned, or by the army of stout men he had at his command. He wanted to marry someone who *truly* loved him.

This, he realised, was quite the tricky task, so he sought out the wisest of the wise women in the land and demanded her advice.

'The only way to tell if a wife truly loves you,' she told him, 'is to let her go. If she loves you, she will return.'

This the rich and powerful man interpreted in his own rather cruel fashion, for such is the nature of rich and powerful men.

He ordered the most skilled carpenters to erect a wooden platform the same height as the highest tower in his magnificent castle, which, with him being so rich and so powerful, was very high indeed.

Once completed, he ordered the most skilled painters to paint the platform so cunningly that, when you stood at the window of the highest room in the highest tower, it would look like you were standing at a door that opened out onto a sweeping meadow, stretching to the distant horizon, rather than dangling over the edge of a hundred-foot drop.

Thus prepared, the rich and powerful man took his first wife.

Theirs was a simple celebration followed by a meal no better than that which the bride of a blacksmith or a potter might expect, for he did not want her to be swayed by his great riches.

As evening fell, they ascended the highest tower to a bare bedchamber, devoid of trappings and unattended by servants, for he did not want her to be swayed by his power.

In the morning, just as dawn was breaking, he flung open the windows and showed her the view of the glorious meadow beyond.

'Wife,' said the rich and powerful man, 'if you do not love me, truly love me, then for both of our sakes, now is the time to leave.'

The wife trembled. 'Oh master, oh husband,' she said, 'what would people say?'

'They will say we were not well suited. Do not fear; I grant you your freedom and I will send a trunk of gold after you, so that you will never want for the rest of your life.'

The wife weighed this promise of gold against the meagre fare that had been their wedding meal. She weighed her freedom against her enforced betrothal to a man she neither knew nor cared for. She watched the meadow flowers welcome the first rays of morning, thinking how lovely they were, and how such simple pleasures would be even more enjoyable with a small sum set aside and a free choice of husband.

She gave her spouse of half a day a half-smile and then, stepping out into the meadow, fell to her death in the eight foot space between the painted platform and the high tower wall.

The rich and powerful man tutted and shook his head. True to his word, he ordered his servants to drop a trunk of gold out of the same window, which landed a short distance from her twisted and lifeless body, before being returned unopened and only slightly damaged to his treasury.

The very next day, the rich and powerful man set about searching for his second wife, telling all that listened that his bride had been unworthy and had taken her own life. He did not feel any remorse, for that is not the way of rich and powerful men. He reasoned thus: his wife had had the best part of an evening and an entire night to get to know him. If she, given the choice, had left him for a mere trunk of gold, then she could not have truly loved him and so deserved her entirely self-inflicted fate.

His second bride soon joined his first in the castle graveyard and, when his third and fourth swiftly followed, he had his courtiers draw up a list of all the eligible women of the land so that he might have his next bride lined up even before the latest one took that fateful step out of the tower's high window.

His brides heard rumours of what had happened to those who went before them. When offered the choice of freedom, they also believed they were being offered life. Whatever had made the other wives unworthy, whatever had made them take their lives, surely it lay in the uncertain future, perhaps when their cold and distant husband demanded his conjugal rights.

A few wondered why the other wives had not made the same choice? Maybe some had, and the promised chest of gold had bought their silence. A few wondered, idly, sleepily, how it was that the tower they thought they'd slept in was now at ground level. But the painters of the meadow had been cunning indeed and the secret of the platform was closely guarded.

In time, dulled by repetition, the rich and powerful man became even more callous. He would make no effort to woo his wives and would even deliberately behave boorishly. He was convinced that true love would be able to see through to his true self, to his true nature, and would forgive this ugly subterfuge.

In time, the demand to give a daughter's hand to the rich and powerful man would cause great grief in each household he approached. Distraught parents knew that the day after the wedding they would be mourning their daughter's closed coffin. Even so, none could refuse the rich and powerful man, for all knew just how rich and powerful he truly was.

In time, a line of red ink was struck through the names of all of the available women of high birth, of high wealth or of high beauty in the land. As his one hundred and fifty-eighth wife was laid to her rest, a courtier humbly apologised that, as far as he could see, there was nobody of suitable standing left in the land to marry.

The rich and powerful man glared at this attendant with barely controlled anger. 'Fool! What care I for standing? For wealth? For manners? Draw up a new list! Find me every marriageable girl in the land. And find me a new wife by tomorrow!'

The courtier bit his tongue, thinking of the dowries that the rich and powerful man had demanded from each of the previous wives, thinking of the young men of breeding who had long since left to seek brides in foreign lands, there being none left in this one. It might have been nice to know that the rich and powerful man would have accepted a commoner a little earlier than this. But he merely bowed his head and sent for the latest census.

In the modest home of the rich and powerful man's one hundred and fifty-ninth bride-to-be, the bride's father, a widower and farmer, wept and cursed the day his only daughter had been born – for what would become of him once she joined the other one hundred and fifty-eight wives in the rich and powerful man's overflowing castle graveyard?

His daughter did her best to reassure him. 'Fear not, father, for I will not go easily to my doom. I shall do all that I can, all that I must, to avoid it.'

'But the wedding is tomorrow!' her father protested. 'What can you possibly do in so little time?'

The bride-to-be thought on this for a moment. She was an uncommonly intelligent young woman, but not so full of herself that she would not seek help. 'I shall do what I always do when I do not know the answer,' she said calmly. 'I shall walk until I find a person who does.'

And so she set out, her stomach knotted with worry, for truly, how could she expect to survive when so many women before her had perished? Surely it would be best to carry on walking, never to return home at all. But then, what would be the fate of her father, of her village? What terrible wrath would the rich and powerful man bring down upon them for her selfish actions?

It was in this distracted state that she realised she had left the path far behind. Her heart thudded. Was she lost? This was not somewhere she had ever been before – she wasn't even sure which way she had come. A thin thread of smoke drifted up between the trees and eagerly she followed it to neat little cottage in a clearing.

'Yes?' A querulous voice made her jump. 'What do you want?'

The bride-to-be spun round and saw an old, stooped woman hard by her elbow. 'Ah!' she exclaimed. 'How quietly you snuck up on me!'

The old woman smiled an enigmatic smile. 'I did not sneak up on you, child. I was here all the time. You merely did not notice.'

The bride-to-be opened her mouth to argue, but then stopped herself and stayed silent. The crone's smile widened and her eyes sparkled.

'Here,' she said, handing the bride-to-be a basket of herbs to carry. 'Come into my house. It's not often I get intelligent company.'

As they sat, sipping an infusion made from the freshly picked herbs, the old woman repeated her question, though more kindly this time. 'What is it that you want?'

The bride-to-be could have asked the way back to the path. She could have asked her host where she might find the wisest woman in the land. But instead, she began to tell her tale of woe.

The crone listened, her heart hardening. Even in her younger days, she might have struggled with a task such as the one her visitor was describing. How could this slip of a girl ever hope to escape the fate that had descended upon her? The old woman had heard of this rich and powerful man, and what happened to his many wives. What manner of man, she had often thought, would play this evil game? She stirred her tea, watching the leaves swirl, trying to think of the kindest way she could to tell the young woman that her future was, alas, sealed.

Suddenly she snapped to attention. 'Child! *What* did you just say?'

'The only way to tell if a woman truly loves you,' the bride-to-be repeated, 'is to let her go. If she loves you, she will return.'

'And?' The crone trembled as she asked it.

'And that is what the rich and powerful man says during each of his wedding ceremonies. The next morning, his wife is found dead, seemingly by her own hand.'

The wise woman carefully placed her cup down, despite the turmoil she felt. Those were *her* words, echoing back at her from across the years; how had they been warped to such evil intent? This was not a problem she could ignore.

'The path,' she said after a moments' thought, 'is a short way beyond the well to the right of the gate. I promise your problem will be tackled by the wisest mind in the country. Return home, child. I will bring news before the day is done.'

When the bride-to-be had gone, the wisest of wise women in the land set out for the castle of the rich and powerful man to see what preparations were being made for the wedding day, and to see what exactly the rich and powerful man had done with her long-ago advice.

*

The farmer's daughter was out fetching logs as dusk fell, bringing in twice as many as were needed for she did not know if she would ever do this task again, when she realised the wisest of wise women stood silently by the fence, watching her.

'Wise woman,' the bride-to-be said humbly, 'do you bring me hope?'

The wise woman nodded. 'I do. Tell me, child, do you have three gold coins?'

The bride-to-be looked at her in surprise. 'We are not a wealthy family, but we will pay you all that we have, and the rest as soon as we can.'

'I'm sure you would, dear, but you'll need those coins much sooner than that.' She rooted in her purse. 'Here. Make sure the clothes you are to be married in have a good hiding place for these. Now, how far can you jump?'

Again, the bride-to-be looked at her in surprise. 'Ah, about seven or eight feet, I suppose.'

'Well, which is it? Seven or eight? I need hardly say that I would not be asking were it not of vital importance.'

The bride-to-be nodded solemnly. 'Seven.'

The wise woman scratched behind her ear. 'Well, I think we can get it moved that far. Now, listen very carefully and make sure you do *exactly* as I say.'

*

On the day of the wedding, the father of the one hundred and fifty-ninth bride tearfully said goodbye to his one and only daughter and the weeping townsfolk escorted her to the waiting carriage, certain they would never see her again.

The simple ceremony proceeded as it had one hundred and fifty-eight times before and, as the plain wedding repast was shared in the room at the top of the tower, the newly-wed found herself wondering at this boorish man who sat before her and determined to find out his true nature. The rich and powerful man was hesitant and more than a little surprised; for over a year now, his brides had all been timid little things, all too eager to take that early-morning offer of escape that unwittingly sealed their fates. This one was sharper, more perceptive and, it seemed, genuinely interested in him, for all his distant manner and blunt behaviour. As the evening wore on and the candles burnt low, he found himself opening up to her.

But while the rich and powerful man warmed to his bright new bride, she thought of all his other wives and of the indifference with which her new husband spoke of those who had sat on the same plain, wooden chair she sat on now. It was his wealth and power that had allowed him to become such a cold-blooded monster and to escape the consequences of his evil deeds.

The rich and powerful man spoke through the night. At dawn, stuck in a routine of his own devising, he threw open the tower's window with a heavy heart. His bride looked out at the painted meadow, seamlessly blended into the early morning light, and smiled at her new husband, holding out a delicate hand to him. 'It looks so lovely. Will you come with me?'

He stared at her, confused. 'Ah, no. But if you don't love me...' He trailed off as she took a step away from him and then, her dress fluttering in the wind, she ran forward and leapt out of the window. He quickly turned to avoid the unpleasant sight and sound of her demise and sighed. He'd never had a wife run out of the window before and he had so hoped that this one was different, that she would be the one who chose not to leave him, and so proved her love was true.

Still, he thought, he'd been right to expand his net to those born of lower status. He had worried that they would be cowed by his wealth and power, but this one had seemed more interested in him than his treasury. A shame then, that ultimately she had left him, just as they all had, and so fallen to her death.

And then he heard his name called.

'It is lovely!' she said. 'Won't you come out, dear husband?'

He gazed in amazement, for there in the middle of the meadow stood his one hundred and fifty-ninth bride, looking up into the dawn sky.

Suddenly, she stooped to the flower-strewn earth beneath her feet. 'Oh look! A golden coin. I wonder how that got there?'

The rich and powerful man squinted into the half-light and wiped his eyes as she stooped once more and held aloft another two coins. 'They're everywhere!' she laughed. 'Like buttercups! What a miracle!'

The rich and powerful man thought of all those chests that had followed his brides over the years, how damaged some of them were, and cursed his servants for their carelessness. And then, before the rich and powerful man had truly realised what he was doing, he stepped out of the window of the highest tower in his castle and fell to his death, for nothing is as tempting to a rich and powerful man as the lure of more gold, more riches, more power.

The bride, still in her wedding dress, still clutching her veil, wiped away a tear and then carefully climbed down from the platform. The rich and powerful man's guards were astonished when she knocked on the door to the tower, alerting them with downcast eyes to the tragic fate of their lord and master.

And so the one hundred and fifty-ninth bride became the richest and most powerful widow in the land. But not for long. She knew it was her husband's wealth and power that had made him such a heartless beast, and knew that such a future awaited her, if she were not careful.

She gave away the entire contents of his vast treasury to the families of his first one hundred and fifty-eight wives, saving only the three gold coins that belonged to the wise woman.

Her final order, before she disbanded the rich and powerful man's retinue, was for the painted platform to be burnt, and the high tower demolished, putting an end to those symbols of cruelty.

When she returned home on foot, her father embraced her in astonished relief and the village rejoiced well into the night, feasting in honour of her good fortune. But, in the morning they began to whisper: surely she had kept some of the treasure for herself? Why did she not share it with them? Heaven knew they could do with a new well, or another herd of cattle, or some fine clothes. Rumours spread of how she had descended a hundred feet without a scratch on her. People asked themselves what witchcraft had been covered up by the destruction of the castle's tower? How exactly had the great and powerful man come to fall to his death from his lofty perch, and, childless as he was, who would replace him at the castle?

The villagers shook and rattled the door of the farmer's humble home and, bleary-eyed, he pulled it open. He listened to the villagers' concerns, nodding all the while; these were thoughts he, too, had had during the long night. But when they went to his daughter's chamber to demand answers, they found it cold and empty.

By then, the one hundred and fifty-ninth bride was already a moonlit night's walk from her village, and further still from the rubble of the tower and the smouldering remains of the painted platform.

By then, she was well on her way to becoming the wisest woman in the land.

Late

Well really! Anyone can see that *I* should have been the hero. An elegantly dressed white rabbit, making haste along the river bank, fearing he's late... Ah, but late for what? And hurrying where? Dear Reader, doesn't that just grab your attention?

Instead, that chit of a girl follows me. As if *that's* an inciting incident! And what a frightfully weak character: a tearful child with terrible vocabulary, barely able to think for herself. Have you read her inner monologues? Uncommon nonsense. Wrong-headed, self-obsessed, always going on about her wretched cat.

How under earth did *she* become the focal point of the story? I know, a minor character can sometimes steal the show, but that's when the character is *interesting*!

Having thrust herself rudely into the spotlight, she runs around at the whim of a scatterbrained author. 'Drink me,' the bottle says, so of course, she does. 'Eat me,' the cake says and does she even stop to think about the calories?

She drinks and eats, eats and drinks, shrinking and growing like a pair of badly maintained bellows, getting herself in a right muddle, always forgetting to pick up that damned key.

How hard can it be? It's a *key*. Pick up the key, drink the potion, go through the door and out into the garden.

How can *anyone* stretch that out until the end of Chapter Seven?

You can tell the author hasn't a clue what to do with her either; lurching from one scene to another, padding it out with mixed-up nursery rhymes and mangled poems, demanding answers to the same questions the baffled Reader might ask, such as 'Where shall I begin?' and 'Which way I ought to go from here?'

Whereas I had a beautiful story arc. Full of drama and

excitement, an epic love story at its beating heart. And one that didn't need a waking-from-a-dream ending.

Instead, I end up as a mere recurring theme, my appearances reduced to prodding Alice down the narrative path. Drop my fan *here*, send her over *there,* heroically try to impose a little order in the courtroom. All of which adds up to a big fat nothing, as far as the telling of *my* story goes.

And the love interest? Mrs. Rabbit gets elbowed aside for thinly disguised caricatures of Alice's barely more tolerable siblings and incomprehensible riddles without answers.

Oh, it's my own fault, in the end. That's the worst of it! It was all down to the chaotic way the author works, conjuring up oddball characters and throwing them into the mix like shuffling a deck of cards. Little wonder he's not brave enough to use his real name.

Plenty of rhyme but no reason.

Early on in the proceedings there was a kickoff meeting where the strongest voices could emerge, the major and minor characters would be refined, and some semblance of plot cobbled together.

Only, I wasn't there. Not until long after the best roles had gone.

Damned Hatter, damned March Hare, telling me that butter was good for my pocket watch. Butter! I should have realized they were trying to delay me, to wrangle *their* parts into something bigger. Page hogs. They're about the only thing Alice gets right: it is quite the stupidest tea party.

So now you know.

When I run around saying I'm late, *that's* what I'm late for.

But perhaps all is not lost. There's going to be a sequel, a second chance to tell my tale. Not underground this time, alas; but I'm sure there's still a significant role for a rabbit of my undoubted talents. The planning meeting is today. About now, actually.

Heavens! Oh my! Is *that* the time?

The Burden

The traveller shouldered his burden and carefully adjusted the straps. The load was unforgiving and he had a long day's walk ahead of him.

Other than the weight wrapped in thick cloth and fixed to his back, he carried little. The road would provide. A small water skin, an empty purse tucked into his sleeve, and, of course, his axe.

He took his lunch – a bowl of rice and a bean stew reheated too many times to tell what beans they once were – with an old woman, who welcomed him into her roadside shack, offering him sustenance in return for chopping her firewood.

Her prattle slowed and then died as he lowered his pack and briskly set about his task, the close grain pattern of the ji chi mu making the wood dense. The old woman was lucky to have such off-cut pieces, too gnarled or split for the local carpenters to use. It would burn slowly, so he cut the lengths short.

When there were no more logs to chop, he warmed down by steadily honing the sharp edge of his blade, a sheen of sweat matting the grey hairs against the cord-like muscles of his arms. They ate in silence, the old woman's wooden spoon rattling in her unsteady hands.

'Who are you?' she asked as he got up to go, looking in fear at the stone slab he hefted onto his back.

He smiled in return. 'Really. You wouldn't want to know.'

*

Salt stung his eyes. The water skin he'd refilled at the old woman's was empty and he felt himself start to stumble on the uneven path as it snaked upwards. The coast was a long way distant and these hills were not cooled by the breezes that stirred the chimes and swayed the lanterns of Fuzhou, the life he had left behind. Ahead, shimmering in the distance, a stand of bamboo promised at least some respite. He'd rest a while, wait until the heat of the day had eased before continuing his journey.

But as he approached he saw that the stand was already occupied and when the three men there rose with languid ease, he heard at his back the soft shuffle of the footsteps of a fourth.

'Well,' said their leader, all swagger as he took up position in the middle of the dusty road. 'What is it that weighs you down so, granddad?'

'It is of no value to you,' the traveller replied.

'We'll be the judge of that,' the leader said, his voice hardened. 'Let it drop!'

So he did, tugging on the knots that set it free, stepping forward as it slammed into the baked earth, drawing a sharp yelp from the bandit who had been creeping up behind him. As the weight was lifted from his shoulders he stood up taller and felt the lightness that comes when you release a great burden, felt as if he could float away from the ground. A sensation that would not last long, he knew, but which always seemed to last as long as it was needed.

'Fancy axe, old timer,' the leader said. 'Where did you steal that from?'

'I was given—'

'Ah, you know what? I don't care. Just hand it over.'

He heard the sound of ripping fabric from behind him, heard the sudden intake of breath. Heard the fourth bandit's tentative 'Um... boss?'

'I can't do that,' the traveller said.

'No?' The leader cast dagger eyes at the bandit crouched behind the impudent traveller, wondering what he was waiting for.

'No,' the traveller agreed.

The bandit laughed a hollow laugh and drew his ox-tail sword, the wrap on the grip faded and uneven, the curved surface dull and pitted, a blade older than the man waving it angrily in the air. 'You're crazy. We have swords! We outnumber you,' he said.

'Still.'

'Are you so prepared to die, old man?'

'My tombstone is ready,' the traveller said. 'Is yours?'

*

When it was over, the traveller tapped the blade of his axe on the shoulder of the fourth man, who was still bent over the engraved slab of grey stone, still tracing the deeply cut characters. He looked up, in fear and wonder.

'You... were the Emperor's executioner?'

'Yes,' the traveller said, feeling the stretch in his shoulders and arms, just as he had in the courtyard of the Winter Palace, as the gong struck to announce the dawn and the end of a man's life. And, just as it had that mist-shrouded day, his axe measured the distance to the bandit's neck. He nodded at the tombstone. 'He had that made along with his own, had it sent to me the night before. I think he hoped I would not be able to go through with it, that it would unnerve me. But it did not. I did my duty.'

'So now?'

'Now I travel,' he said. 'I walk the roads and paths of Minyue and keep them clear of bandits such as you. Men stupid enough to prey on an old hunter, such as I. This is my penance, a small deed to negate the chaos of these troubled times. One day, I will be too slow, too old, and it will be me who falls. When I do, I ask only that the Emperor's parting gift be mounted at my head.'

The bandit lowered his eyes, a splash darkened the stone, whether sweat or a tear the traveller could not tell. 'And me, laoshi?'

He lifted the axe, leaving a red triangle on the bandit's flesh. 'You were not fool enough to draw your weapon, not fool enough to attack me from behind. So. Perhaps you will go home, spread the word that this is no country for bandits. Perhaps you will live to a ripe old age. Perhaps. If you run.'

The bandit ran.

The traveller cut a large square from the thick cloth of the leader's cloak and wrapped it around the tombstone, replacing the one that had been torn. With the material that remained he cleaned his executioner's axe, carefully wiping away every trace of blood. Then he knelt beside each of the fallen men, whispered a few words into the hot stillness, before patting them down and half filling his purse from their pockets. He did not take it all, little though there was: even bandits have families, even bandits deserve a decent marker for their graves.

He looked around the stony plain, wearily peering into the haze filled distance. It would not do to linger, not here, where the three men now lay. He sought out their water skins, felt their lightness, turned them over one by one, draining the scant drops before casting them aside with a sigh and once more lifting his burden.

No water, but still.

The road would provide.

Tigg Montague's Ponzi Pyramid Scheme

He counted the stack of coins on his desk, sorting them as he did. The larger piles were a dull brown, some tinged with green: copper farthings, ha'pennies, and pennies; all well used. Of silver coins there were few, of half-crowns there was but one. Carefully, he noted the total in his ledger and then, leaning back, rubbed a bony hand across his chin and sighed.

It was going to be a thin Christmas.

The chests that had taken so long to fill had taken a far shorter time to empty. True, the contents were technically out on loan and the repayment of even a small part would make him financially assured. But that wasn't the way it worked: what little came back went straight out again, the need far greater than his reserves.

As for interest; none of the poor he lent to were in a position to pay even a penny in the pound.

There was, it seemed, no profit in being good.

Ebenezer Scrooge had a serious cash-flow problem.

'Humbug!' he cried, and an elderly dog staggered up from its place by the fire, coming to rest its head on his knee. The tattered ears, the hind leg at an awkward angle, spoke eloquently of a brutal life, until Scrooge had taken pity and rescued him. If, at the time, he had done so only to bring joy to a distraught Tiny Tim, nevertheless the dog had returned the favour and affection with more interest than any of his other investments. Tiny Tim, now thankfully not so tiny, the best and most expensive doctors in London having worked miracles, was away at boarding school and Scrooge's only relative, his nephew Fred, had emigrated with

142

his entire family to America, the passage paid for with heavy heart by Uncle Ebenezer. Humbug was the most steadfast and loyal of his few companions.

Though, as Scrooge's belly rumbled at the fading memory of his meagre repast, even that friendship would be sorely tested if his money and food ran out.

Still, he consoled himself, look at what he had accomplished along the way. All in Marley's name, of course, though as Marley had been dead these last ten years, died ten years ago that very night, it was perhaps obvious that the charitable deeds came from Scrooge's own hand, though few knew the reason why; the memory of his former business partner's chains, the life debt that Scrooge hoped he could in some way help pay off.

And he had, hadn't he? Or at least, he'd *tried*. Why, only that morning, he had saved another poor wretch and his sizeable family, fallen on hard times, or harder than usual. Cold, hungry, but determined to live better lives, desperate to celebrate Christmas as it should be.

He hoped his good intentions wouldn't be tripped up by gambling, drinking, and, alas, whoring. With every loan Scrooge entreated the recipient to avoid any and all Spirits, but he'd already had to write off a disturbing amount of such debts and had oft thrown good money after bad, to keep the poor that crossed his path away from prison, away from the workhouse.

Perhaps there were sounder investments... But he'd baulked at that when it was so obvious his wealth could do so much good elsewhere. How could he stand by, when many thousands were in want of common necessaries; hundreds of thousands were in want of common comforts?

Such as Mr Jones and his indeterminate number of dependants. Why, the man had been so distraught he seemed to forget exactly how many kids he had, and their ages, and their names. Scrooge had felt a flood of sympathy for the man, obviously unused to pleading his plight, and, though it had left his purse severely lightened, he had pressed what coins he could into the man's grimy hand, wishing him a merry Christmas and a more profitable New Year.

And then he'd watched, anxiously, as Mr Jones had crossed the yard to the local tavern and disappeared into the smoky rooms within.

Oh, there had been some successes, he supposed. Companies kept afloat and now positively booming, from Todd's Barbers to Mrs Lovett's Pie Shops. Even his one-time clerk, Bob Cratchit, was now an up and coming businessman, a beneficiary of Scrooge's generous patronage.

But these were advances to tradesmen and professionals; men and women who knew the value of hard work and sobriety. For the rest, his loans had spectacularly failed to lift them out of their poverty. It was shocking how many of those who came to him, cap in hand, telling their depressingly familiar tales of woe, ended up being knifed in bar brawls a scant day or so after he had given them a generous long-term sum on virtually no interest. Money which would never be repaid, not in this life, anyway.

And so, a scant three years after his Yuletide epiphany, things were beginning to look rather bleak.

Odd to remember that moment of giddy exultation, the almost drunken feeling of relief to rediscover his festive cheer. The sensation had quietened down to a benevolent generosity as the year rolled by, only to flare back into life each Christmas since, inspiring ever grander acts of charity.

Not this year though. Desperate times were upon him.

The sound of the oversized door knocker reverberated through the old house like thunder, startling Scrooge out of his reverie, sparking a feeling of ominous dread.

But it wasn't the ghost of Jacob Marley on the step; it was Bob Cratchit, dressed in a sharp new suit and cravat, an ebony walking cane in one hand and, in the other, a page of cheap print, the rough paper mottled, the letters badly set, the crudest of publications.

'I thought you ought to see this, Ebenezer.'

Scrooge took it for a song sheet at first, the sort that were traded on the street three for a penny, but as he read his brow creased.

'What is this, Bob?'

'Instructions.'

'Instructions? For what?'

'For getting the best terms on a loan. From you.'

'But—'

'It's all there. The trigger phrases, the ideal number of kids; not so many that the case appears hopeless, but enough, and young enough, to tweak at your heart strings. A family fallen on hard times, an appeal to one more fortunate, the assurance that, if they can just be helped out this once, they'll be able to turn the corner and live a more honest and profitable life. With special appeals for winter and, of course, for Christmas.'

'I'm... being played?' Scrooge said in disbelief.

'I assumed you knew *that*,' Cratchit said, eyebrow raised. 'I wanted to make sure you knew the industrial *scale* of it.'

*

Scrooge went to bed that night thinking unseasonally dark thoughts. He'd read and reread the page of instructions, comparing them to the recent appeal by "Mr Jones", presumably not his real name, not if the first instruction had been followed. A surprise, then, to find at the bottom of the sheet the brazen signature of its author, one Montague Tigg, a notorious ne'er-do-well, as responsible as any pub landlord for the crushing poverty of his fellow man.

As he contemplated cold revenge, the bell tolled one and a spectral figure thickened out of the gloom at the end of the bed.

'Scrooge!' intoned the ghastly ghost, 'We hoped we were done with you. Thought we'd turned you to the light. Are ye having doubts?'

'Yes,' admitted Scrooge.

'Tush! And you, one of our success stories! What ails you, man?'

Scrooge edged to one side, trying to look behind the apparition's dark cloak. 'Are you on your own?' he asked.

'Yes, and we're all on double shifts. It's a busy night.'

'But you can speak?'

'Aye, that I can,' said the Ghost of Christmas Yet to Come. 'Though with first visits, it's more dramatic if I don't. And it's all about the drama, the shock to the system, y'ken? Plus, my accent...'

'Well, anyway, I'm glad you're here.'

'Are ye?' the Ghost said, doubtfully.

'You see, I have a few questions.'

'Mr Scrooge! That isn't the way this goes, and ye know it.'

'Bah. Tell me Ghost of the Future; look into mine. Six months from now. Do I continue to do good?'

There was a moment's silence. And then the spirit sucked in its breath. 'Ah, I see.'

'Is it as bad as I feared?'

'Worse. Much worse. Oh dear. That you should come to this...' the spooky figure shook its head, bones rattling as it did.

'But that's just one possible future, isn't it?' Scrooge said, sitting up tall. 'They're not fixed? *You* showed me that.'

'Well, yes.'

'So, show me a better future?'

'It doesn't quite work that way–'

'The horse races perhaps. Who wins the next Derby?'

'Mr Scrooge! What you ask we cannot – *will* not do. It's hardly ethical, is it now? Why, I might as well tell you to clear out of railway stocks, or teach you the dark arts of pyramid insurance scams, or Ponzi schemes.'

'Ponzi schemes? What... what are they?'

'You're missing the *point*, Mr Scrooge. We're forces for Good, for the light. I'm not gonna see you go back to being the mean old miser you once were!'

'Nor would I,' Scrooge protested, 'Mankind is my business, now. Rest assured I'll continue with the charitable deeds.'

'That's as may be–'

'Which I can hardly do if *I'm* in the poorhouse, can I?'

'Well, 'tis most irregular, but there's some sense to what you say. It is the rich and greedy who tend to fall foul of these dastardly schemes.'

'There you go then! Think of it as a Robin Hood tax. Money taken from the rich and given – with a judicious hand – to the poor. And, if you're in any doubt, look again to my future, Spirit, the one where you tell me about these... financial irregularities, and see that I am true to my word, see that I continue to freely share what comes my way. What say you?'

*

In his fireside bed Humbug stirred, chasing rats, for he knew nothing of rabbits. Life was good. And getting better. Visited by his own ghosts that evening, he'd seen visions of walks in foreign lands, his master by his side.

He couldn't understand what Scrooge talked about on those long walks; subprime mortgages and Dot Com bubbles, long term capital management and Enron, Black Wednesday and Brexit? Nor why Scrooge now traded under a new, seemingly respectable name: Tigg Montague, but that really didn't bother him. The sun warmed his old bones and the rich men his master met seemed awfully keen to make friends with Humbug, patting his head and offering him titbits under the table, as if by winning him over they might somehow win his master over as well.

Humbug wagged his tail in his sleep. The titbits were rich, but no richer than the marrow-filled bone he now knew Scrooge had bought him for Christmas Day.

*

So, there you have it. As we lurch from financial crisis to financial crisis, it seems Scrooge, or his ghost at least, has rather a lot to answer for. And God bless us, every one!

ValCon

By now into its third year, ValCon was the biggest computer games convention on the circuit. Bigger than E3, bigger even than GamerCon, tickets sold out faster than Glastonbury, despite their equally hefty price tag.

Naturally, I wasn't a paying punter. Do I *look* like a gaming nerd? I'd been hand-picked from the High and Mighty Modelling Agency to be one of the Valkyrie: a cohort of Amazonian women kitted out in strips of leather and impractical armour. It was our job to issue passes for the night's festivities.

The passes were what it was all about.

You couldn't get into Valhalla without one.

And, this being Valhalla, you had to die a glorious death to gain entry.

But most importantly of all, we Valkyrie had to be paying attention. Which turned out to be the tricky part. In my high-heeled thigh-length calfskin boots I towered above the dweebs milling around me and with a chest-plate even more impressive than what nature provided, the demands for selfies, for dates, and of course, for Valhalla passes, was near constant. As for the garish battles plastered across the exhibition centre's roof-high screens that we were supposed to be watching...

Well. Let's just say once you've seen one game of WarCraft, you've seen them all.

Little wonder it was a lottery rather than a meritocracy. Little wonder I gave my passes to those select few tall enough and brave enough to look me in the eye and not drool.

But then, gaming skills weren't really the point. The reason the players played, the reason they came to the Con in the first place, was because the all you can eat and drink victory feast was a reward for *lucky* heroes.

If you had to be the best player to gain entry, then the cavernous expo centre would have been a ghost town. That anyone and everyone could, with the roll of a Valkyrie's dice, be picked for glory, was what encouraged even the most hopeless geeks into ever more stupid acts of online bravery.

Normally, I'd run a mile rather than spend any social time with the special needs nerds, but it irked me that we Valkyrie weren't invited to the evening entertainments. Even if it was just so I could sneeringly turn them down.

It was probably an equal disappointment to those gamers who assumed – or at least hoped – that the Valkyrie were part of their prize.

We didn't even know what the feasting hall looked like. The doors were kept closed during the day and the ValCon posters, asking 'Will YOU Gain Entry To Valhalla?', unsurprisingly featured a clutch of us Valkyrie, or rather, last year's equally statuesque models.

It was shrewd marketing: as long as Valhalla stayed hidden and mysterious people would aspire to win entry, however lame it actually turned out to be. They'd keep coming, keep buying the merch, keep playing the stupid and expensive games.

But y'know? Curiosity. The not knowing was getting to me and if it had that effect on a seasoned events-campaigner and computer game-phobe like myself, what pure intoxication it must have been for those barely pubescent youths who spent every waking hour bathed in the light of their twin 28-inch computer screens.

The convention was a three-dayer, kicking off on Friday for the industry boffins or those without regular employment, and culminating with a grand finale on Sunday evening. I'd pretty much resigned myself to thirty hours at minimum wage with maybe a few usable shots for the portfolio, so to find, as Sunday's 'game over' rang out, an aged sheet of parchment waiting for each of us in the dressing rooms was a surprise I hadn't prepared for.

An invitation to the final Valhalla feast.

We girls looked at one another.

'Can't,' said Nadine, our leader, six-six with jet black hair down to the small of her back. 'Kids.'

I breathed a sigh of relief. Stood next to her, I risked looking kinda *average*.

'Vegan,' shrugged Paula, and with those two down I became the tallest Valkyrie still in costume.

I appeared to think on it for a moment. '*Might* be good for networking,' I suggested, 'Besides, after spending the last three days on my feet, I'm famished.'

And so, at 6.07pm, three Valkyrie marched up to the feasting hall, scattering mere mortal men in our wake. I pounded my fist on the surprisingly solid doors. I figured, since we were still in costume, we'd best continue to play the part. Flanked by Red Sonja and the incongruously named Daisy, it was beholden on me to be utterly imperious, regal, and aloof. To look down on all and sundry.

That part, at least, came naturally.

Fortunately, by luck or because the stocky guards had a keen appreciation for the theatrical, my hammering was immediately greeted by the doors swinging open. We strode in, followed by an eager horde of awe-struck gamers.

I have to admit, as I cleared the entrance and the vista opened up, even I had to bite back a breathless 'wow!' The hall was spectacular, all dark beams and wooden shields. Low tables surrounded a central fire pit – an *actual* fire pit, how the hell had they managed to get that past Health and Safety? – flames and ash and sooty smoke that softened the distant walls and made the whole feel both larger and more enclosed at the same time.

The oak floor was strewn with fur rugs and the occasional

cushion or bolster for those for whom sitting crossed-legged was too painful. At each table sat a Viking warrior in full rig: all leather and scarred torsos and impressive facial hair. I don't know which agency they came from, but they certainly looked the part and were obviously there to help guide proceedings.

Best of all, there wasn't a single computer screen in the whole blessed hall, which, after three days in Nerdsville, was welcome relief.

At the top table, watching proceedings with a scowl and an eye patch, sat the largest of the warriors, playing Odin. The dude probably filled in for Santa in the wintertime and no doubt scared the shit out of any little kids unfortunate enough to find themselves sat on his muscular knee.

He beckoned us over. Except, when I looked round, Sonja and Daisy had already been whisked off to the tables either side, so I guess he beckoned me over.

'Sit!' he commanded, his voice rumbling like a log-jam.

I sat, trying to keep my back as straight as possible, while making sure my chain-mail skirt covered my lap from the attentive gaze of the lank-haired youths who ended up across from me.

'Eat!'

A man of few words, our Odin.

But, as the platters of meat and bread, and as goblets of honey-sweet liquid were forced upon us, I was happy to oblige. The little computer twerps sprawled, tongues lolling, as I regaled them with tales of heroic exploits lifted straight from Xena: Warrior Princess.

As I basked in their adulation and the food kept on coming, I was wondering how to guarantee myself admittance when ValCon rolled around once again next year, when I became acutely aware that the hall had fallen silent, all eyes turned to me.

Only, not me. Odin, at my side, was now standing, his tree-trunk legs glistening barely a foot away.

'Valkyrie!' he hollered, and then gabbled something in a language I didn't recognise.

I found myself being pushed into the cleared centre of the hall, along with Sonja and Daisy.

Whether their Viking escorts had translated for them, or maybe I was just slow on the uptake, Sonja was suddenly airborne, wrapping her lithe body around one of the timber supports, doing an energetic pole dance that left me exhausted just watching, the spectacle made all the more impressive when I considered the high risk of splinters.

The hall erupted in cheers as she descended for the last time to the floor, though Odin sat impassive and glowering.

Daisy shook her head. Juggling an apple, a tankard and a carving knife, she somehow ended up slicing the apple in mid-air, catching each falling sliver in her mouth.

And then she stood grinning, knife between her perfect teeth, tankard balanced on the blade, tilting her head towards me in contemptuous challenge.

The next thing I knew, I was holding a spear snatched from the nearest wall, as Daisy paled and backed away.

At school, before I discovered boys and before they discovered me, I was big in athletics. Literally. Taller and stronger than even the guys. I could have had a future, my PE teacher said, bemoaning my lack of commitment while standing in a convenient spot to look down my burgeoning cleavage. I was good at high jump, long jump, and not bad at middle distance sprints. But most of all, I excelled at the Javelin.

True, that had been fifteen years ago and the spear in my hand wasn't anything like the smooth aluminium spike I was used to, and maybe all that mead had gone to my head, but heck, who doesn't want to put on a show?

Realising what I was about to do, there was a sudden exodus from the table at the far end of the hall. I hesitated a moment, half hoping to be stopped, but Odin just nodded, keeping his one eye squarely on me.

I hefted the spear, feeling its weight, allowing my hand to

travel towards the centre of gravity, trying to pick a target. Up in the rafters, carvings of a wolf and an eagle presented themselves, but felt wrong, somehow. As did the goat and the animatronix crows. I shuddered to think what the insurance bill would be if I impaled one of *those*.

And then I spotted a large barrel suspended in the lower eaves, the end painted red with a white centre.

Not wanting to over-think it any further, I took three paces back then strode the same distance forward and let fly.

It was a fluke, of course. The modern Javelin is a 'how far can you throw', rather than an accuracy, event. Hitting the keg was nothing more than luck. Hitting it dead centre, a splintering crash that sent foaming mead cascading to the table below, where nerds and warriors quickly jostled to catch it in cup or mouth, was the equivalent of winning the lottery. I was engulfed by a cheering mob before being deposited, slightly giddy, before Odin.

He nodded and grinned and proffered a horn full of some nectar even sweeter than the mead we'd been drinking. Why they didn't give up on all the stupid computer games and just sell booze, I'll never know.

Odd, the way time seemed to stretch after that. If we Valkryie wore watches or carried mobile phones, I'd have checked to make sure I wasn't going to miss the last tube home, but the feast showed no signs of letting up, though Daisy and Sonja had slipped away at some unnoticed point. The gamers at Odin's table seemed to come and go; a stream of fresh spotty faces.

Odd too, that I never got totally drunk, or totally full, despite the endless supply of food and drink. Odd that each time Odin stood and another spear was thrust into my hands, there was always a new keg to aim at.

Oddest of all, was that Odin's garbled speech began to make sense. Whether it was through repetition, or what, I finally pieced it together.

'Heroes fit the age into which they're born!' he bellowed, to an audience of even younger looking geeks than when first we'd sat down, complete with metallic contact lenses and tattoos in the shapes of computer circuits.

I *say* I understood Odin's speech: I get the words, at least. As for the meaning... I'll have to ponder that, as the feasting goes on forever.

Bad Day

In the distance, the last baleful rays of the setting sun paint the mountains a glistening red. Or perhaps they are on fire. Or bleeding. In the fading light it's hard to tell.

As I Back away from the slavering beast, the wet ground beneath my heels crumbles and with a lurch I look down to the stormy waters below. Stormy waters broken by thrashing limbs, glistening suckers, and razor-sharp beaks. Great. Just great. And I'd really thought my day couldn't get any worse.

I take a sideways step onto firmer ground and duck as a ghostly form wails down from above. Between the advancing hellhound, the banshee flying through the gloomy night air, and the host of sea monsters waiting far below, there isn't a heck of a lot of space left for me. I tap the gizmo around my wrist, willing it to glow green. No such luck. It stays stubbornly dark, an unknown and possibly unknowable force blocking the emergency teleport signal.

Taloned claws catch at my hair and I'm enveloped in musty, graveyard air. I shrink away from the banshee's soul-sapping touch and the coal-fire eyes of the hellhound flick upwards. It seems the wailing woman has his attention as well.

As the banshee sweeps in once again I reach out, grab a cold, bony limb, shout 'here boy!' and toss it over the cliff. The beast bounds past, mouth agape, all puppy-dog enthusiasm, a thick trail of saliva hitting me wetly in the face as its teeth wrap around the screeching banshee and they plunge together to their tentacular doom.

There's a moment's blissful silence and I dare to hope that maybe, just maybe, I might survive this ordeal after all.

Assuming I can find a spot where my teleport works, while it still has enough juice to get me out of here.

'How *terribly* uncouth,' a discorporate voice hisses each word in alternate ears as a black-winged form flickers in and out of existence. 'Now I'll have to think of an even *better* ending...'

ABOUT ARACHNE PRESS
www.arachnepress.com

Arachne Press is a micro publisher of (award-winning!) short story and poetry anthologies and collections, novels including a Carnegie Medal nominated young adult novel, and a photographic portrait collection. We are very grateful to Arts Council England for financial support for this book and three others, a tour round the UK and our live events.

We are expanding our range all the time, but the short form is our first love.

The Solstice Shorts Festival
(http://arachnepress.com/solstice-shorts)
Now in its third year, Solstice Shorts is all about time: held on the shortest day of the year on the Prime Meridian, stories, poetry and song celebrate the turning of the moon, the changing of the seasons, the motions of the spheres, and clockwork!

The Story Sessions
(http://arachnepress.com/the-story-sessions)
We showcase our work and that of others at our own bi-monthly live literature event, in south London, which we run like a folk club, with headliners and opportunities for the audience to join in.

We are always on the lookout for other places to show off, so if you run a bookshop, a literature festival or any other kind of literature venue, get in touch; we'd love to talk to you.

Follow us on Twitter: @ArachnePress @SolShorts

Like us on Facebook: ArachnePress, SolsticeShorts2014, TheStorySessions

MORE FROM ARACHNE PRESS
www.arachnepress.com

BOOKS

Short Stories

London Lies
ISBN: 978-1-909208-00-1
Our first Liars' League showcase, featuring unlikely tales set in London.
Stations: Short Stories Inspired by the Overground line
ISBN: 978-1-909208-01-8
A story for every station from New Cross, Crystal Palace, and West Croydon at the Southern extremes of the East London branch of the Overground line, all the way to Highbury & Islington.
Lovers' Lies
ISBN: 978-1-909208-02-5
Our second collaboration with Liars' League, bringing the freshness, wit, imagination and passion of their authors to stories of love.
Weird Lies
ISBN: 978-1-909208-10-0
WINNER of the Saboteur2014 Best Anthology Award: our third Liars' League collaboration – more than twenty stories varying in style from tales not out of place in *One Thousand and One Nights* to the completely bemusing.
Solstice Shorts: Sixteen Stories about Time
ISBN: 978-1-909208-23-0
Winning stories from the first *Solstice Shorts Festival* competition together with a story from each of the competition judges.

Mosaic of Air by Cherry Potts
ISBN: 978-1-909208-03-2
Sixteen short stories from a lesbian perspective.
Liberty Tales, Stories & Poems inspired by Magna Carta
ISBN: 978-1-909208-31-5
Because freedom is never out of fashion.
Shortest Day, Longest Night
ISBN: 978-1-909208-28-5
Stories and poems from the *Solstice Shorts Festival* 2015 and 2016.

Poetry

The Other Side of Sleep: Narrative Poems
ISBN: 978-1-909208-18-6
Long, narrative poems by contemporary voices, including Inua
Elams, Brian Johnstone, and Kate Foley, whose title poem for
the anthology was the winner of the 2014 *Second Light* Long
Poem competition.
The Don't Touch Garden by Kate Foley
ISBN: 978-1-909208-19-3
A complex autobiographical collection of poems of adoption
and identity, from award-winning poet Kate Foley.
With Paper for Feet by Jennifer A. McGowan
ISBN: 978-1-909208-35-3
Narrative poems based in myth and folk stories from around the
world.
Foraging by Joy Howard
ISBN: 978-1-909208-39-1
Poems of nature, human nature and loss.

Novels

Devilskein & Dearlove by Alex Smith
ISBN: 978-1-909208-15-5
NOMINATED FOR THE 2015 CILIP CARNEGIE MEDAL.
A young adult novel set in South Africa. Young Erin Dearlove has lost everything, and is living in a run-down apartment block in Cape Town. Then she has tea with Mr Devilskein, the demon who lives on the top floor, and opens a door into another world.
The Dowry Blade by Cherry Potts
ISBN: 979-1-909208-20-9
When nomad Brede finds a wounded mercenary and the Dowry Blade, she is set on a journey of revenge, love, and loss.

Photography

Outcome: LGBT Portraits by Tom Dingley
ISBN: 978-1-909208-26-1
80 full colour photographic portraits of LGBT people with the attributes of their daily life – and a photograph of themselves as a child. @OutcomeLGBT

All our books (except poetry books) are also available as e-books.